Majid Schumacher

A TALE OF HERITAGE, HEARTBEATS, AND THE PURSUIT OF DREAMS

PAVAN ARORA

ISBN 979-8-89475-333-1

Contents

CHAPTER 1

New Beginnings and Goodbyes

The magistrate's room was filled with an air of solemnity as the judge's voice resonated through the space. "The court grants the divorce between Mr Tapinder Singh and Ms Tracy Vain". The declaration hung like a heavy curtain, signalling the end of a chapter spanned over two decades.

The room was awash with various emotions; each person, including Sarah, processed the announcement in their own way.

At 21 years old, Sarah possessed a captivating blend of Indian and American heritage. Her physical appearance was a harmonious fusion of features reflecting her diverse background. With a radiant smile, expressive eyes and hair styled that glanced an aura of youthful energy.

But today, she sat there with a heavy heart, sadness and resignation. As the gavel struck, her parents' marital bond was severed, and she couldn't help but feel a deep ache.

Her parents, Tapinder Singh and Tracy Vain, parted ways after 23 years of marriage. They had built a life together, overcome hurdles, and succeeded, yet now they were walking separate paths.

The chill of the New York winter seeped into the room, adding a tangible weight to the sombre atmosphere. Sarah's emotions mirrored the frosty weather outside. Her gaze remained fixed on the judge, but inside, she grappled with her own turmoil. Her eyes, usually full of vivacity and life, were now clouded with tears that threatened to spill over at any moment.

Beside Sarah, Tracy's face was a mixture of sadness and relief. The years of tension and disagreements had taken their toll, but the finality of the divorce was still a heavy burden to bear. She exchanged a glance with Tapinder, a man who had been her partner in business and life. The love they had once shared had now transformed into something different, yet the history they had created together remained a part of them.

The legal proceedings continued, formalities were discussed, and the lawyers engaged in professional dialogue. Tapinder's gaze remained on Tracy, his former partner and now ex-wife. He couldn't help but reflect on their journey together, from humble beginnings to creating a multimillion-dollar business. He knew this decision was right for both of them, yet a pang of sadness gripped his heart.

As the proceedings ended, Sarah couldn't contain her emotions any longer. The tears that had welled up finally streamed down her cheeks. The reality of the situation was overwhelming. Her parents, once a united front, were now separate entities. She rose from her seat and left the magistrate's room, her steps heavy and her heart heavier.

Outside, in the corridor, Sarah's suppressed emotions broke free. She leaned against the wall and let herself cry, the weight of her recent breakup compounded by the dissolution of her parent's marriage. She had always seen her parents as pillars of strength; now, that pillar had crumbled.

Tracy followed her daughter out of the room, giving her space to grieve. She had seen Sarah grow into a mature and understanding young woman, often wise beyond her years. But today, she was a daughter needing comfort, not a confidante in their shared struggles.

After what felt like an eternity, Sarah's tears began to subside. She straightened herself, wiping her tears away with her hand. Tracy approached her, her heart aching for her daughter's pain.

Without a word, Tracy enveloped Sarah in a warm embrace. Sarah hesitated momentarily before returning the hug, their bond reaffirmed by their shared sorrow. The two women stood there, mother and daughter, drawing strength from each other during a storm.

"I'm sorry, Sarah," Tracy whispered, her voice choking with emotion.

Sarah stepped back slightly and looked at her mother. Tracy's eyes were red, and her makeup was smudged from her tears. At that moment, Sarah realised that her mother was not just her parent but also a person with her own vulnerabilities.

"It's okay, Mom," Sarah said softly, her voice quivering. "We'll get through this."

Tracy managed a small smile. "Yes, we will."

They stood momentarily longer, letting their unspoken words hang in the air. Then, Tracy took Sarah's hand, leading her back into the magistrate's building. The lawyers were wrapping up the final details, and Tapinder waited patiently outside, his eyes red but determined.

Sarah looked at her father, his presence a source of comfort and complexity. He had been her hero, guiding her through life's challenges. As they faced this new chapter, she couldn't help but wonder what the future held.

Tapinder noticed them and walked over, his face a mixture of concern and care. He hugged Sarah, holding her tightly as if shielding her from the world's pain. Sarah felt a mix of emotions—the comfort of her father's embrace and the realisation that even he, with his strength and wisdom, was not immune to life's trials.

"We'll be okay, Tape," Sarah said, her voice muffled against his shoulder.

Tapinder pulled back slightly, cupping Sarah's face in his hands. "I know you're strong, Sarah. And I know you'll always make us proud."

Sarah nodded, her tears now mingling with a smile. "I love you, Dad."

"I love you too, princess," Tapinder said, his voice breaking with emotion.

Tracy joined the hug, completing the circle of love and support. In that moment, amidst the challenges and heartaches, they found solace in each other's arms. The path ahead was uncertain, but they would navigate it together – a family redefined but unbreakable in their bond.

The cold winter air seemed less chilling as they left the magistrate's building. The weight of the divorce decree was still present, but their shared love and determination were stronger. It was a new beginning, not just for Tapinder and Tracy but also for Sarah.

After leaving the magistrate's building, the family gathered at their favourite restaurant to mark the end of one chapter and the beginning of another. The atmosphere differed from the courtroom—casual chatter, subdued laughter, and the clinking of glasses filled the air.

As they settled into a booth, Tapinder raised his glass. "To new beginnings," he proposed, a sincere but somewhat weary smile on his face.

The clinking of glasses resonated, but as the evening progressed, the tone shifted. Tapinder was drawn into more serious conversations despite his attempts to keep the mood light. He took a moment to address the elephant in the room.

"I know this is a lot to take in," he began, looking at Tracy and Sarah, "but I want you both to know that this divorce doesn't change our commitment to the business. We've worked hard to build what we have, and I believe we can continue to run it successfully, even if we're not married anymore."

Tracy nodded in agreement, her eyes reflecting both sadness and determination. "Tapinder is right. Our professional partnership can endure, even as our personal one transforms."

The conversation shifted to Sarah's future. Tapinder, with a hint of paternal pride, said, "You're incredibly talented, Sarah. Have you thought about pursuing your MBA?"

Sarah contemplated the question, her mind torn between furthering her education and joining the family business. "I'm considering it, Dad. But I also want to contribute to what you and Mom have built."

Tracy interjected, "Sarah, the business will always be here. Pursuing your MBA might open new doors for you to bring fresh perspectives to the company."

Amidst the discussions, the glasses were refilled, and the mood lightened. However, as the night wore on, Tapinder's jovial demeanour gave way to a more sombre tone. He insisted on driving them home, dismissing the concerns voiced by Tracy and Sarah. "I'm fine," he slurred slightly, the effects of alcohol evident. "I've done this a thousand times. Trust me."

Despite their protests, Tapinder stubbornly got behind the wheel.

The drive started in silence, each passing streetlight casting shadows on the strained expressions of the two women in the car. Sarah nervously glanced at her father, weaving between lanes, clearly under the influence. Fear gripped her heart as she pleaded with him to pull over or let Tracy drive, but he paid no heed.

Tragedy struck at the intersection of fate and poor decisions. Another car, oblivious to the impending disaster, collided with them. The world twisted into chaos — the screeching of metal, shattering glass, and the deafening silence that followed.

When Sarah opened her eyes, disoriented and dizzy, the first thing she saw was the wreckage of the car. Panic set in as she looked around for her parents.

Battered and bruised but conscious, Tracy reached out to Sarah with trembling hands. The realisation of their survival brought a wave of relief mixed with grief.

Then, amid the wreckage, they found Tapinder. The warmth of his embrace from earlier that evening was replaced by the cold reality of loss. Tracy cradled his lifeless form, tears blending with the rain that had started to fall.

Emergency services arrived, rushing the family to the hospital. The news of Tapinder's death echoed through the sterile corridors. Tracy held onto Sarah in the hospital waiting room, their grief merging into a shared pain that no court decree could ever sever.

As they faced the devastating consequences of that ill-fated night, the remnants of their shattered family clung to each other in the cold hospital room, grasping for strength in an unforeseen tragedy. The road ahead, once uncertain, now stretched into an unknown future, forever altered by the events that transpired after what was meant to be a new beginning.

CHAPTER 2

Gathering the Pieces

In the days that followed Tapinder's funeral, the hospital's sterile atmosphere gave way to the cold reality of grief. Tracy and Sarah sat in a quiet corner of a coffee shop, nursing their sorrow with steaming cups and hesitant conversation.

Tracy, with a heavy heart, broached a topic that had been lingering in the air. "Sarah, there's something I need to tell you," she began, her voice tinged with sadness. "Apart from us, your father had someone in his life, someone he cared deeply for. Her name is Elizabeth."

Sarah looked up, surprise etched on her face. "What? How long?"

Tracy sighed. "It started a few years ago. Tapinder and Elizabeth found solace in each other. He wanted to tell you himself, but..." She trailed off, unable to hide the pain of missed opportunities.

A mixture of emotions danced on Sarah's face – surprise, confusion, and hurt. "So, there's someone else."

Tracy nodded. "Yes, but remember, it doesn't diminish what we had as a family. Elizabeth was there for him when things were tough. We should try to understand and respect that."

As they navigated the complexities of their personal lives, the conversation shifted to the professional realm. A meeting was scheduled at the company headquarters, where Tracy and Sarah faced the challenge of maintaining stability amidst personal upheaval.

The boardroom, which had witnessed countless strategic discussions, was tense. Flanked by lawyers and a team of top executives, Tracy sought a delicate balance between grief and responsibility.

"Tapinder's vision was what built this company," Tracy began, her voice steady. "And though he's no longer with us, his legacy lives on. We need to ensure that the business continues to thrive, just as he would have wanted."

Sarah, who had taken a more active role in the business in recent years, nodded in agreement. "Dad always emphasised the importance of family and stability. I'm committed to upholding that legacy."

Tracy continued, "Elizabeth will be a part of this transition. Tapinder believed in her abilities, and we owe it to him to give her the support she needs. She will now lead Marketing for Singh-Vain Inc. to make it America's #1 grocery retailer."

The room buzzed with grief and determination as plans were outlined to maintain the company's trajectory.

Despite her struggles, Tracy exuded a strength that inspired those around her. Amid it all, Elizabeth entered the room with quiet resilience. Tracy acknowledged her presence, emphasising the need for unity in moving forward.

As they discussed strategies and transitions, the focus remained unwavering—the business Tapinder had poured his heart into. They found a semblance of normalcy in those conversations, a shared commitment to honouring his legacy.

Tapinder Singh's journey to success began with humble roots in India. Driven by a vision for a better life, he ventured to the United States, landing a job as a salesman in a small grocery store in New Jersey. There, he honed his business acumen, learning the ins and outs of the grocery industry.

His dedication and innovative ideas caught the eye of Tracy Vain, a young and ambitious marketing specialist who frequented the store. Tracy recognised Tapinder's potential and proposed a partnership to change their lives. They eventually got married, combining their skills and aspirations.

Pooling their savings, Tapinder and Tracy took a bold leap and opened their first grocery store. Their commitment to quality, customer service, and innovative marketing strategies propelled their business forward. The couple worked tirelessly, expanding their venture into a chain of successful grocery stores.

Tapinder's keen understanding of the operations and Tracy's marketing finesse transformed their business into a thriving enterprise. The Singh-Vain chain of grocery stores became a household name, known for its diverse offerings, competitive prices, and commitment to community engagement.

Their success was not only measured in financial terms but also in the lives they touched. The business flourished, employing hundreds of people and becoming an integral part of the communities it served. Tapinder and Tracy, once newcomers with a dream, had built an empire that impacted not only their lives but also the lives of those they employed.

Their journey was a testament to hard work, perseverance, and the power of partnership. Tapinder and Tracy's story embodied the American dream realised through shared determination and unwavering commitment from a small grocery store in New Jersey to a flourishing retail chain nationwide.

CHAPTER 3

India Calling

The distant echoes of a bygone era reverberated in the Singh household as if the walls themselves held the memories of a love that had once flourished within. The photographs adorning the walls bore testament to happier times – family gatherings, vacations, and the radiant smiles of Tapinder, fondly known as Tape. But now, those smiles were relics of the past, preserved in frames.

The aroma of spices wafted through the air, hinting at the Indian dish that Sarah was preparing. As she stirred the pot, she lost herself in thoughts that spanned the years. Her father's departure had left an indelible void, and Sarah often found herself wishing for his guidance—a wish that would forever remain unfulfilled.

Tapinder had always seen potential in her and encouraged her to pursue her dreams without reservation. His absence reminded her that even the strongest bonds could be severed, leaving behind fragments of memories and unanswered questions.

Tracy's presence brought Sarah back to the present. Her mother's footsteps were accompanied by the clinking of plates and the soft hum of conversation. Sarah looked at Tracy, her eyes reflecting a mix of emotions. Here was a woman who had weathered storms and forged ahead, prioritising the company's success over her heartache. It was a strength that Sarah both admired and struggled to comprehend.

"Smells delicious," Tracy said, her voice carrying a warmth that transcended the boundaries of their altered reality.

Sarah offered a smile. "I am trying the new masala concoction we have prepared in-house."

Tracy nodded, her gaze distant yet contemplative. "Great, looks like it should work!"

As they sat down to eat, the conversation flowed – a blend of updates, plans for the business, and the occasional reminiscing of moments they had shared. Sarah's heart swelled with a mixture of love and melancholy.

Here they were, a mother and daughter navigating a new chapter together, united by blood and circumstance.

After dinner, Tracy approached Sarah solemnly. "Sarah," she began, her voice tinged with sadness, "we need to talk about your father's family in India."

Sarah looked at her, puzzled. "Dad never really spoke about them. I thought he had lost contact."

Tracy sighed, her eyes reflecting a more profound sorrow. "He did, Sarah. Before we married, Tapinder broke all connections with his family and country. Your grandparents were against our marriage and wanted Tapinder to marry a local Indian girl back home. It's a painful chapter I never fully understood, but now, it's our responsibility to inform them about his passing."

Sarah, taken aback by this revelation, nodded understandingly. "But how do we even begin? And what about the memorial service here?"

Tracy explained, "In Hindu traditions, it's customary to immerse the deceased's ashes in the Ganga. Your father's ashes need to find their way to the holy river. It's a journey we must undertake, Sarah. To his town, Behalpur, in India."

Sarah's initial reaction was resistance. "Mom, it's tradition, but we have much to handle here. Going to India seems too much for the memorial service and the business."

Sarah, still apprehensive, continued, "And Dad cut ties with India. Why should we go there now, especially when he consciously decided to leave it behind?"

Tracy explained gently yet firmly, "Your father's decision to disconnect was complicated, Sarah, and we may never fully comprehend it. But this journey is not about the past; it's about finding closure and respecting the essence of who he was. We must see this through, not just as a family but as individuals who loved him."

As Tracy spoke, Sarah noticed the determination in her mother's eyes, a reflection of the strength that had carried them through the highs and lows of their family's journey. Tracy continued, "And this trip is not just for him but for us. It's a chance to connect with a part of him that we may not fully understand. Please, Sarah, consider it a final act of love for your father."

Gradually, Sarah's resistance softened. She looked at Tracy, her initial objections giving way to a reluctant acceptance. "Okay, Mom," she finally conceded. "Let's go to India—for Dad."

At that moment, a silent understanding passed between mother and daughter, a shared commitment to honour the man they had lost and embark on a journey that would, in some way, help them find closure amidst the echoes of the Ganga's sacred waters.

As they began preparing for their journey, the reality of the cultural pilgrimage ahead settled on them. The trip to Behalpur would bridge the gap with Tapinder's past and immerse them in rich Indian traditions. It was a poignant chapter in their lives, a journey of closure, and an opportunity to pay homage to the man who had left an indelible mark on them.

CHAPTER 4

Princess's Wish

The dawn of a new day brought a whisper of hope, a glimmer of unexplored possibilities. Sarah sat by the window, watching as the first rays of sunlight painted the sky in hues of gold and pink. The morning breeze carried a sense of renewal, a reminder that life was in constant motion and that there was space for new beginnings even amidst the trials and tribulations.

As Sarah sipped her morning tea, her thoughts turned to the conversations of the previous evening. The echoes of the past had woven a cloud of emotions, and within the threads of memory, there lay a yearning that had remained unfulfilled – a yearning to connect with the roots that had shaped her existence.

"Good morning, sweetheart," Tracy's voice broke through Sarah's reverie as she entered the room, a smile on her lips.

"Morning, Mom," Sarah replied, setting down her cup. "I was thinking..."

Tracy raised an eyebrow, her curiosity piqued. "About what?"

Sarah hesitated for a moment before gathering her thoughts. "After immersing father's ashes, I want to see Dad's childhood home and stay with his family for some time."

Tracy's expression softened as she sat down beside Sarah. "Princess, I understand your feelings, but it will depend on your father's folks welcoming us to their home. After what your father did, I am not sure if they would be keen to welcome us."

Sarah's eyes welled up with tears, and she wiped them away with the back of her hand.

Tracy placed a comforting hand on Sarah's shoulder. "I think it's a beautiful idea, sweetheart. Your father would have appreciated it. Let's hope for the best."

Sarah smiled through her tears, grateful for her mother's support. "I feel like it's a way to honour him, to give him closure. And maybe, in doing so, I can find some closure too."

Tracy pulled Sarah into a gentle embrace, holding her daughter close. "You're stronger than you know, Sarah. And I'm here with you every step of the way."

Sarah and Tracy began preparing for their journey to India in the following weeks. The prospect of travelling to a land that was both unfamiliar and a sense of belonging stirred a mixture of emotions within Sarah.

She researched their ancestral town, learned about its customs and traditions, and even picked up a few basic phrases in Hindi.

Tracy meticulously crafted a letter for Tapinder's family, her hopes tethered to the paper as she sealed the envelope.

"Sarah, I'm sending this letter to your grandfather, Joginder Singh, in Behalpur. I found his address in Dad's visa papers from two decades ago. I am informing them about Tapinder's passing and telling them we'll be coming to Haridwar to immerse their son's ashes." Tracy explained, her eyes reflecting a mix of anticipation and uncertainty.

"What if they don't reside there anymore, Mom?" Sarah voiced the concern that lingered in the back of her mind.

"It's a possibility, darling. That's why I've also booked a hotel for us in Haridwar. I've reached out to them, hoping they can assist us on the journey to the Ganga river bank near Haridwar for the immersion," Tracy shared in her tone, a blend of determination and practicality.

Do we have their phone number? Sarah inquired.

"Tapinder's diary listed a few phone numbers. I attempted to call them, but they appear to be out of service," Tracy replied.

As the day of their departure drew near, Sarah felt a mixture of excitement and trepidation. She had known her grandparents through stories and photographs, but meeting them face-to-face was a step into the unknown. Sharing the news about her father's passing was daunting and necessary, a bridge that needed to be crossed.

CHAPTER 5

India - The Beginning of the Journey

With 30 minutes to land, Sarah's heart raced with nervousness and a newfound sense of purpose. Tracy's hand found its way to hers, providing a reassuring anchor amidst the uncertainty.

The long flight had left Sarah and Tracy weary, their bodies yearning for the sensation of solid ground beneath their feet. As the plane descended towards the New Delhi Airport, the vibrant landscapes of India unfolded beneath them – fields stretching out like a patchwork quilt, monuments standing as silent witnesses to history, and bustling streets that seemed to pulse with life even from a distance.

Sarah peered out the window, her eyes capturing the fleeting glimpses of the country she had heard stories about but had never seen. "Tracy, look to your right," she exclaimed, pointing towards a sprawling sports ground. "It's incredible how much we can see from up here!"

Tracy joined her daughter in gazing at the panoramic view, a sense of wonder lighting up her tired eyes. The anticipation of reuniting with family and embarking on a journey of self-discovery filled the air around them.

As the plane touched down and the cabin lights flickered on, Sarah's excitement became a question. "Who's coming to receive us, Tracy?"

Tracy offered a reassuring smile, her voice calm. "I sent our flight details to your dad's family. Let's hope they have sent someone to pick us up. Otherwise, we'll book a taxi and go to Haridwar directly."

Tracy and Sarah went through immigration, collected their bags and swiftly exited the airport. They started looking around for anyone holding a placard with their names. After a long wait, they were disappointed that no one had their names.

"We'll have to activate Plan B, Sarah," Tracy said sadly. She continued, "We'll go to Haridwar, and from there, I have told the hotel guy to help us arrange to go to the banks of the river Ganga."

Amidst the bustling crowd at the airport, a young man stood holding a placard that read "Sarah & Tracy." He arrived late, his nerves fluttering with excitement and anticipation. As he checked his watch, he couldn't help but feel a sense of responsibility for this critical task.

Sarah and Tracy started dragging their luggage behind them when Sarah did a final scan of the arrival lobby, searching for a familiar face or sign. She was glad to see – a placard held by a perplexed young man.

As their eyes met, Sarah tilted her head in curiosity. She made her way towards him, a mixture of determination and amusement on her face. The young man felt his heart race faster as the girl approached, her head still tilted.

Without missing a beat, Sarah reached out and gently turned the placard upside down to read the names. A smile tugged at the corners of her lips as she realised the mix-up.

The young man's nervousness melted away as he laughed at his mistake. "Are you Sarah or Tracy?" he asked, his smile infectious.

Sarah laughed, too, her energy contagious. "I'm Sarah," she replied, her amusement evident. "Nice to meet you, Mr. Placard Holder."

"I'm Majid, the driver for Joginder Ji. Welcome to India." Majid's cheeks flushed as he introduced himself.

Tracy joined them, a warm smile on her face. "Thank you, Majid. We appreciate you coming to pick us up."

Sarah looked at Tracy and smiled, "Mom, this is a good start with our family. If they have arranged our pickup from the airport, I am sure they will allow us to stay with them."

Majid gestured towards their luggage. "Let me help you with these."

He swiftly took Tracy's bag off her shoulder and helped Sarah with hers. They exchanged thanks, and as they made their way out of the airport, the awkwardness of their initial encounter seemed to dissipate.

"Hope you had a good flight," Majid said, conversing.

Tracy nodded. "It was long, but we're excited to be here."

As they strolled towards the parking area, Majid continued to weave a narrative about the affluent Singh household in Behalpur, masterfully transformed by Joginder Singh's unwavering dedication and hard work.

Majid shared the unique dynamics of the Singh family: " The family reminds me of Bollywood movies. In an era where nuclear families were becoming prevalent in the bustling cities of India, Joginder Singh Ji remained committed to preserving the tradition of a joint family, fostering a sense of togetherness that transcended the boundaries of modern urban living."

Sarah and Tracy were amused by Majid's talk.

Sarah enquired, "How long have you been working with Joginder Singh Ji?"

Majid smiled warmly, "I've been a part of Joginder Singh Ji's household since childhood. Joginder Singh Ji supported my education, and with his encouragement, I am pursuing my dream of starting my own business."

As they reached the car, a sleek Mercedes, Sarah couldn't help but admire it. "Wow, my grandfather has a great car," she quipped.

Majid chuckled. "Well, it's my pride and joy too. I take good care of her."

"By the way, you both have come at the right time," Majid said with a twinkle in his eyes. Joginder Singh Ji's granddaughter Neetu is getting married in a few days, and the Singh Home is all decked out for the wedding."

Hearing this, Sarah and Tracy exchanged glances, contemplating whether their presence might dampen the family's festive spirits.

Majid was a young man of striking presence, his physique reflecting his vibrant spirit and unwavering determination. Standing at an above-average height, he carried himself with an air of confidence that was approachable and reassuring.

Broad shoulders hinted at the strength beneath his casual demeanour, a force that had served him well in his various roles—be it as a driver, a helper, or a friend. His muscular arms were often tanned from spending time under the sun, a testament to his dedication and hard work.

His complexion bore the sun-kissed glow of someone who spent significant time outdoors. A sprinkling of freckles across his cheeks adorned his skin, a charming reminder of the hours he'd spent in the open fields. His rugged features were softened by a warm, easy smile that could light up a room, making him an instant favourite among those he encountered.

Majid's hair was a dark, unruly mop that seemed to have a mind. It fell in waves around his forehead and ears, giving him an endearing, almost carefree appearance. His fashion sense was simple and practical, reflecting his active lifestyle. Majid's attire blended comfort and style in jeans and a casual kurta.

Majid's physical structure embodied his spirit—a blend of strength, warmth, and determination that endeared him to everyone he met. His presence was magnetic, drawing people in with his genuine nature and the untamed spark that spoke of his dreams and aspirations.

The midday sun bathed the landscape as Majid expertly navigated the car through the bustling streets of New Delhi. Sarah and Tracy settled in the backseat and gazed at the city's vibrancy.

Sensing their curiosity, Majid began unravelling the chapters of his life. As the car hummed along the highway towards Behalpur, Tracy initiated the conversation. "Majid, there's something about your journey that intrigues us. How did it all begin for you?"

Majid, focused on the road, delved into his past. "I lost my father when I was just thirteen. With two younger sisters to look after, I stepped into the responsibilities that life thrust upon me. It was tough but forged my determination to overcome any challenge."

Majid shared snippets of his life, his dreams, and his aspirations. "You know," he said excitedly, "I want to open my car garage on the Delhi-Dehradun Expressway. Apart from repairing cars, I will convert normal cars into sports cars because car racing is my passion. Joginder Singh Ji tells me that my father, a car mechanic, kindled his passion for car racing in the Singh household."

Amused by Majid's story, Sarah remarked, "That's incredible, Majid. How did you find your way in cars amidst all this?"

Majid leaned back, reminiscing, "Like my father, I found solace in working with cars. A local garage was owned by a friend of Joginder Singh Ji, who allowed me to watch and learn there. Soon, I was fixing minor issues, and my fascination became a skill."

Sarah, genuinely interested, inquired, "So, you're self-taught?"

Majid nodded, "Yes, I would observe the mechanics at work, ask questions, and experiment on my own. Cars became my passion and my way of contributing to the family. Eventually, I became Mr. Joginder Singh Ji's right hand for cars."

Impressed by Majid's journey, Sarah smiled, "That's incredible. It's more than just a skill; it's a story of determination and passion."

Majid nodded, "Indeed, it is."

The car rumbled along the highway, the hum of the engine harmonising with Majid's narrative. The journey to Behalpur became more than a physical distance covered; it was a passage through the landscapes of Majid's life, each mile revealing a layer of resilience and determination.

As the car glided along the highway, Sarah, intrigued by Majid's passion for cars, asked, "Majid, tell us about your car racing adventures?"

Majid's eyes lit up with excitement and nostalgia as he began sharing his racing journey. "Oh, the thrill of the racetrack! I've been assisting Jolly Bhaiya for a few years now. I have learned much by helping Jolly Bhaiya compete in car races."

"The roaring engines, the smell of burning rubber, and the cheering crowd—it's an experience that words can't quite capture."

Sarah couldn't help but express her surprise when she learned he didn't race himself. "Majid, you seem so passionate about cars. Why don't you race?"

Majid responded with a glint of passion, "Well, I'm more of a behind-the-scenes guy. I assist Jolly Bhaiya in the racing scene."

Tracy, curious, chimed in, "Assist? What exactly do you do?"

Majid: "Everything from fine-tuning the engines to strategising race tactics. Jolly Bhaiya trusts me to handle the technical side, and it's an honour."

Sarah, impressed, smiled, "So, you're the secret weapon behind the victories?"

Majid chuckled, "You could say that. The joy of seeing our car zoom past the finish line is reward enough for me."

The conversation continued, weaving tales of speed, passion, and the camaraderie that defined the popularity of racing car sports in India.

Majid continued, "Over time, Jolly Bhaiya and I faced challenges, learned from defeats, and savoured victories, each race adding a chapter to the story of the Singh home.

We are gearing up for the dangerous mountain race near Dehradun, a coveted event that promises glory and fierce competition."

Sarah exclaimed, "Wow! A dangerous mountain race! That sounds incredibly thrilling."

Majid's eyes lit up, and he chuckled, "Oh yes, this mountain race is a legend here. The race is notorious for its treacherous turns, steep cliffs, and unpredictable weather, making it one of the area's most challenging and dangerous races."

Majid continued excitedly, describing the race, "Sarah, the mountain race is not too far from Behalpur. It's not your typical smooth racetrack. The route winds through the mountains, with hairpin turns and narrow stretches. Many seasoned drivers have hesitated to participate because of its danger. Some didn't make it to the finish line."

Sarah, intrigued, asked, "Is it that risky?"

Majid nodded, "Yes, it is. The terrain is unpredictable, and the weather can change in an instant. It's a true test of a driver's skill and nerve. But, you see, that makes it so appealing to someone like me who dreams of racing. The risk, the challenge—it's all part of the thrill."

Tracy leaned forward, curious. "But Majid, have you ever considered participating as a driver? You seem like someone who lives and breathes racing."

Majid's gaze remained fixed on the road ahead. "I've been saving up to import parts from Japan. Building a proper racing car takes time, and I want to ensure I have the best machine. Anyway, I get to assist Jolly Bhaiya in all the races."

Tracy asked, "Who is Jolly Bhaiya? We've been hearing his name a lot."

Majid replied, "Jolly bhaiya is Joginder Singhji's grandson."

Tracy pondered, "Sarah, so Jolly will be your cousin-brother, right?"

Majid looked confused and asked, "You are part of Joginder Singh's family, is it?"

Tracy replied with a slight smile, "Yes, Majid. I am Joginder Singh Ji's daughter-in-law, and Sarah is his granddaughter from the United States."

Majid's expression softened as he spoke, "I've heard so much praise for Tapinder Singh Ji from Joginder Singh Ji and Amarjeet Aunty. But strangely, no one else seems to talk about him. How is he doing, and where is he now?"

Tracy's eyes took on a contemplative gaze, and a hint of sadness lingered in her response, "Tapinder...he's no longer with us. He's gone." The weight of the words hung in the air, and for a moment, there was a profound silence as Majid processed the unexpected revelation.

To lighten the moment, Sarah interjected, "But Majid, what about racing your car in the competition with what you have now? The thrill of the race, the experience—it might teach you things that a perfect car won't."

Majid sighed, "You don't understand. The competition is fierce, especially with Ravi Chandar, or RC as they call him. He's a phantom who dominates the racing scene. No one has been able to beat him in the mountain race. Not even Jolly Bhaiya."

Tracy said, "But Majid, it's not always about winning. Sometimes, the effort and journey teach you more than the victory itself. You might surprise yourself as a racing car driver."

Sarah emphasised, "Majid, maybe it's time for you to move from the sidelines into the middle of the action!"

Majid pondered their words, his grip steady on the wheel. The notion of participating in the race, imperfect car and all, lingered in the air like an unspoken challenge. The miles to Behalpur seemed to shrink, but the distance to that legendary street race expanded into a realm of possibilities.

The rhythmic hum of the car's engine merged with the ambient sounds of the roads as Majid skillfully navigated through the highway. Tracy glanced at the passing scenery, and Sarah seemed eager for the unfolding journey.

As they neared the ancient city of Haridwar, Majid, with a certain reverence, began to speak, "Har Ki Pauri, the steps leading to the divine Ganga. A dip here cleanses the soul and helps attain Moksha."

Intrigued, Sarah said, "I've always dreamt of experiencing the spiritual energy of this place. Mom, can we make a quick stop?"

Tracy smiled, "Of course, Sarah. Let's make a memory here."

In Haridwar, the trio walked along the sacred ghats. The air was thick with the scent of incense and the distant chants of prayers. As they stood at the water's edge, Majid shared tales of ancient rituals, and Sarah expressed her longing, "One day, I'll take a dip here and feel the sacred waters cleanse my spirit."

Majid took pictures of Sarah and Tracy with the divine river in the background using Sarah's phone.

"You should also come one day in the evening for the Ganga Aarti at Har ki Pauri", exclaimed Majid as they stepped back into the car.

As the car glided through the winding roads toward Behalpur, Sarah, captivated by the landscape, initiated a conversation with Majid about the sacred Ganga.

"Majid, tell us more about the Ganga. How does it start, and where does it go?" she inquired.

Majid, ever the storyteller, began, "The Ganga, the divine river of the subcontinent of India, known to the westerners as the Ganges, originates high in the Himalayas. It's like a celestial journey. The river is born from the Gangotri Glacier, one of the largest in the region and worshipped as Goddess Ganga."

Sarah, intrigued, leaned forward, "From a glacier? That sounds magical."

Majid nodded, "Indeed. It starts small, just a stream, and gains strength as it flows through the terrain. At Devprayag, where Alaknanda joins Bhagirathi, the river acquires the name Ganga. It traverses 2525 km before flowing into the Bay of Bengal. Passing through Rishikesh and Haridwar, it becomes a mighty force, carrying the stories and blessings of the Himalayas."

Tracy added, "And where does it go after that?"

Majid continued, "The Ganga doesn't stop there. It travels across the plains, nurturing the land and its people. It passes through big cities in India like Lucknow, Prayagraj, Patna, and Kolkata. It also crosses through Varanasi, considered one of the oldest inhabited cities in the world. Millions of people find solace on its banks."

Envisioning the journey, Sarah said, "So, it's not just a river; it's like a lifeline for the people."

Majid nodded, "Exactly. And finally, after a remarkable journey of over two and a half thousand kilometres, it meets the Bay of Bengal in the east. The Ganga isn't just water; it's a living entity, a symbol of purity, carrying the essence of the Himalayas to the vast ocean."

Majid added, "There are interesting stories about the river as well. It is said that the River Ganga flowed from Lord Shiva's hair. The place where the sacred river originated is known as Gangotri in present times, and since the river originated from Lord Shiva's Hair, it is also called Jatashankari. Jata means locks of hair."

As the car climbed higher into the hills, the trio found themselves on a physical journey and a voyage through the stories and wonders of the sacred river Ganga.

Looking at the passing scenery, Sarah murmured, "It's more than I ever imagined. The stories, the colours, the spirituality—I can feel it all around. It's like a cultural feast for the senses."

Resuming the journey, the landscape transformed into the lush hills of Dehradun. Gazing at the mountains in awe, Sarah said, "It's like a dream. I never imagined India to be this beautiful."

Majid chuckled, "India is a land of surprises, full of beauty and diversity."

The conversation turned to adventure as they continued.

Majid's eyes sparkled enthusiastically, "A few kilometres from here is Rishikesh, the adventure hub. Rafting, mountain climbing—the thrill is unparalleled."

Sarah, animated, asked, "Have you tried these, Majid?"

Majid grinned, "Not yet. My heart races on the roads, not rivers. But you two can try. It's an experience of a lifetime."

As Behalpur emerged on the horizon, bathed in the warm hues of the setting sun, Sarah, leaning against Tracy, said, "This journey is already more than I hoped for. And it's just the beginning."

Tracy squeezed Sarah's hand, and Majid smiled knowingly, glancing at them through the rearview mirror. The car ascended towards Behalpur, carrying with it the anticipation of new beginnings and the echoes of a shared past.

CHAPTER 6

Heartland Odyssey

The last stretch of roads to Behalpur was a passage through diverse landscapes. As the Mercedes glided through the highways and byways, Sarah and Tracy were treated to sights, sounds, and flavours that painted a vivid picture of the country they were about to explore.

The car cruised along open roads lined with lush fields. The air was filled with the sweet scent of earth and the promise of new beginnings. Sarah watched as the urban landscape transformed into a rural panorama, with quaint towns and local markets dotting the way.

Majid, guiding them through the vibrant journey, suggested a lively roadside dhaba as their first stop. The air was filled with the tantalising aromas of spices and the rhythmic pans sizzle. Sarah, her adventurous spirit ignited, turned to Tracy, "What do you say, Tracy? Ready to dive into the authentic flavours of the region?"

Tracy nodded with enthusiasm, "Absolutely, let's explore!"

Their culinary escapade unfolded with a delightful array of street food – crispy pakoras, mouthwatering chaat, and more.

The dhabba's owner, a genial man with a twinkle in his eye, noticed their intrigue and joined the conversation. "Ah, travellers! You've chosen the best. Our food tells stories," he chuckled, sharing tales of the diverse souls who had graced his establishment over the years.

Majid said, "This is India – a melting pot of experiences, including food!."

As they savoured each bite, the exchange of stories merged seamlessly with the rich flavours, offering them a genuine taste of India's heartwarming hospitality.

Tracy's eyes lit up as she savoured an exceptionally flavorful pakora. "Oh, Majid, you weren't kidding about the food here. This is incredible!"

Majid beamed with pride. "I'm glad you're enjoying it. These dhabas may not look fancy, but they serve some of the most amazing dishes you'll ever taste."

Sarah couldn't help but share her excitement with Tracy. "Did you see how amazing that food was? I mean, those pakoras were like little pockets of heaven!"

Majid grinned, his eyes twinkling. "Absolutely! Indian street food can captivate your taste buds and leave you craving more. And the best part? Each region has its own unique specialities."

Tracy nodded in agreement, her eyes reflecting the satisfaction of a sumptuous meal. "I must say, Majid, you know your way around these places. It's like having a local guide to the best food spots."

Majid chuckled. "Well, I've travelled quite a bit, and I believe that experiencing a place's cuisine is integral to understanding its culture. Food is a universal language that brings people together."

Tracy retrieved a handful of Indian Rupees to settle the bill at the cash counter. "How much for the meals?" she inquired.

The cashier responded promptly, "Not from you, Ma'am. You're the guest of Mr. Joginder Singh Ji."

Majid, displaying a hint of pride, swiftly pulled out his mobile phone, scanned the QR code on the counter, and effortlessly made the payment.

"Digital payment in the hills, that's impressive!" remarked Sarah.

With a smile, Majid affirmed, "Yes, we are ahead of the curve in technology!"

The journey continued, and the road stretched endlessly, flanked by fields and patches of dense foliage. As they approached Behalpur, Sarah felt the undeniable urge for a restroom break.

"Uh, Majid, I need to use the restroom urgently. Can we stop somewhere?" Sarah asked, squirming in her seat.

Majid scanned the surroundings. "It's a bit tricky here. Let me find a spot."

After a few miles, they spotted a cluster of bushes by the roadside. "Perfect," Majid declared, pulling over.

Sarah dashed towards a cluster of bushes, her laughter mingling with the rustling leaves as Majid and Tracy waited in the car, chatting about Behalpur. Little did they know that Sarah's bathroom break would turn into a hilarious escapade.

Suddenly, Sarah's voice pierced the air, "Oh my God! What is that?"

Majid and Tracy exchanged puzzled glances. They turned just in time to see Sarah sprinting towards them, panic etched across her face.

"What happened?" Tracy asked, concerned about furrowing her brow.

"There was a wild pig behind the bushes! It started rushing towards me!" Sarah exclaimed, catching her breath.

Majid and Tracy laughed, the absurdity of the situation sinking in. "A wild pig? Really?" Tracy chuckled.

"I thought I was going to be chased by a pig in the middle of nowhere!" Sarah laughed, the tension dissipating.

Majid, still chuckling, said, "Well, let's find a proper restroom."

As they resumed their journey, fate played a humorous card. They stumbled upon a small motel just a hundred metres down the road. The irony of the situation wasn't lost on them. Sarah, now composed, joined in the laughter.

"Guess the wild pig was just a warm-up for the surprises Behalpur has in store for us," Sarah remarked, wiping away tears of laughter.

As the sun began to set, casting a warm orange glow over the landscape, they found themselves on the final stretch of their journey. The road led them through narrow paths flanked by dense foliage, the sounds of crickets accompanying them like a natural symphony.

Then, amidst the fading light, a signpost appeared – "Welcome to Behalpur." The sight stirred emotions within Sarah and Tracy, a mixture of excitement and a sense of belonging. The town beckoned like an old friend, ready to unfold its stories and secrets.

As the car navigated the town's winding lanes, they were greeted by the warm glow of lamps outside the quaint houses. People went about their evening rituals, casting curious glances at the newcomers. Majid's familiarity with the town was evident as he exchanged greetings with the locals, his presence blending seamlessly with the surroundings.

After a long 7-hour drive, the small town of Behalpur came into view, bathed in the soft illumination of the setting sun behind the mountains.

The car pulled outside a modest yet welcoming house—Joginder Singh's home. The air was filled with anticipation, a feeling that they had finally arrived at the crossroads of their journey.

CHAPTER 7

The Singh Reunion

Majid turned off the ignition, and there was a moment of quiet before Sarah and Tracy stepped out of the car. The town seemed to hold its breath as if recognising the significance of their arrival. As they stood under the vast expanse of the twilight sky, Sarah's gaze met Majid's, a silent acknowledgement of their journey together.

The town had stories to tell, secrets to share, and a connection to offer.

As Sarah and Tracy crossed the threshold into the house, they knew their journey was far from over. The echoes of the past and the future promises converged in this moment, a moment of reunion, discovery, and the realisation that every step taken had led them to this point.

The Singh Home had transformed into a lively hub of celebration. Strings of fairy lights adorned the exterior, casting a warm glow over the courtyard. The air was filled with laughter, chatter, and the faint strains of celebratory music. The fragrance of marigold and jasmine hung in the air, creating an ambience of joy and festivity.

Entering the home, Sarah and Tracy were greeted by the vibrant colours of traditional decorations. The walls echoed with the lively beats of dhol, and the rooms buzzed with the excitement of wedding preparations.

The large Singh Home had seamlessly embraced its new role as a wedding home. Family and friends gathered, sharing anecdotes, reliving old memories, and creating new ones.

As Sarah and Tracy navigated through the lively corridors, they could feel the pulse of the celebration. Each corner whispered tales of love, resilience, and the unbreakable bond that held the Singh family together.

Majid turned towards them with a reassuring smile. "You're about to meet Joginder Singh Ji."

With Majid's words as a gentle push, Sarah and Tracy stepped towards the entrance. The door creaked open, revealing an older woman with kind eyes and a warm smile. She looked at them curiously and familiarly as if their arrival was a long-awaited event.

Tracy extended her hand. "Hello, I'm Tracy, and this is Sarah. We're so glad to finally meet you."

The older woman's eyes held a warmth that transcended the smile on her lips. "I am Amarjeet Kaur, Tapinder's mother. Welcome, my dear." She gently clasped Tracy's hand, inviting her to step further into their home. The genuine embrace in her words carried a depth of emotion, creating an instant connection between the two women.

As they exchanged pleasantries, the scene shifted inside the house. The room was adorned with pictures that captured the essence of generations, stories told through sepia tones and fading colours. And then, he entered the room – Joginder Singh, a figure of authority and love, his presence commanding yet gentle.

Majid stepped forward, gesturing towards Sarah and Tracy. "Joginder Singh ji, these guests have come from afar to meet you."

Joginder Singh's eyes met theirs, a mixture of curiosity and warmth. His voice held a touch of gravitas as he spoke. "Welcome to our home. I hope your journey was comfortable."

Tracy nodded, her voice steady. "Thank you; it was quite the journey. "Thanks for sending Majid. He was a great tour guide for us."

Tears welled up in Tracy's eyes as she took a deep breath, the weight of her words pressing against her chest. "Your town and your home are beautiful. We're sorry to bring you bad news at such a celebratory time in your home."

Joginder Singh looked at Tracy and said, "We cut off all ties with Tapinder after he married you. He also never got in touch with us. It's been 22 years since we last spoke with him."

Sarah's grandmother, Amarjeet Kaur, interjected, "How did it all happen?"

Tears streamed down Sarah's face, her voice quivering with pain and regret. "Dad was driving under alcohol and... met with the accident."

Sarah unwrapped her airbag with delicate hands, revealing an earthen pot cradling her father's final remnants and ashes. Each touch seemed to carry the weight of a thousand emotions, a poignant connection to a past that now rested in the fragile confines of that sacred vessel.

It was a vessel of closure, a container of love. With solemn reverence, she handed the pot to Joginder Singh, their eyes locking in a moment of understanding that words could not capture.

Joginder Singh Ji's trembling hand reached out, and he accepted the pot from Sarah. Their hands touched briefly, a connection that transcended generations. His voice was a whisper, a mixture of sorrow and acceptance. "Tapinder was our blood, after all."

He sank into a chair, his eyes fixed on a photograph on the wall – a snapshot frozen in time, capturing a father and son in an embrace of laughter and love.

Amarjeet Kaur's shoulders trembled as she wept silently, her sorrow mirrored in Joginder Singh's sadness.

After a few moments, a faint smile graced Joginder Singh's lips. "You have your father's spirit in you, Sarah. You've come all this way to share his final journey. That takes strength."

Tears streaked down Sarah's cheeks, her voice quivering. "It's not just his final journey, Grandfather. It's also a new beginning for us, for our family. I hope that, in some way, he's found peace."

CHAPTER 8

Meet the Family

As the sun dipped below the horizon, casting a warm golden glow over Behalpur, Sarah and Tracy surrounded themselves by family. Joginder Singh's home was alive with laughter and chatter, filled with the aroma of traditional Indian delicacies. The extended family had gathered for the wedding.

In the courtyard, Sarah's cousins—Vicky, Jolly, and Neetu—awaited eagerly. They were young and energetic, and their eyes sparkled with curiosity as they looked at the two newcomers.

Satpal Singh and Kripashankar, Tapinder's brothers, stood beside them, their expressions a mixture of curiosity and nostalgia.

As Sarah and Tracy approached, Vicky, the eldest among the cousins, stepped forward with a warm smile. "Welcome to our home, Sarah and Tracy. We've heard so much about Tapinder Uncle. We would love to hear about his great American Dream!"

Jolly and Neetu echoed his sentiments, offering friendly smiles and heartfelt greetings.

Tracy felt a lump in her throat as she realised that Satpal and Kripashankar were the faces of her husband's childhood, the family he had left behind.

Satpal Singh, Tapinder's elder brother, extended his hand to Tracy. "It's good to finally meet you, Tracy. Tapinder often spoke about you before he broke all relations with us after his fight with Papaji."

Tracy's voice was a mixture of gratitude and emotion. "Thank you for having us, Satpal. It means a lot to be here."

Kripashankar, the youngest of the three brothers, spoke up with a twinkle in his eye. "You know, Tapinder was quite the rebel and troublemaker back in the day. Always getting into mischief."

Sarah's eyes lit up with curiosity. "Really? Tell us more about his pranks."

With a playful smile, Satpal said, "Let us tell you about the legendary prank Tapinder almost pulled off in school."

Kripashankar chuckled and recalled the incident: "Oh, that one! Where were all three of us involved? Tapinder lured us into the prank in exchange for cotton candies. For the prank, we kept dead house lizards in the books of a few teachers. It would have been okay until then, but Tapinder got ambitious and placed one in our School Principal's diary."

Satpal interjected and said, "And then there was a slew of screams from various classrooms, including the Principal's room. In those days, there were no CCTVs, but one of our housekeeping staff had seen Tapinder enter the School Principal's room without any reason. Our bags were searched, and a box of dead house lizards was found in Tapinder's bag."

Kripashankar added, "It was hilarious until we were caught. We were in deep trouble. The school called our parents. And we were about to be expelled."

Tracy, amused, asked, "And what did Joginder Singh Ji do when he found out?"

Kripashankar, grinning, replied, "Well, let's just say he pleaded with the principal to let us stay in the school on the pretext of all three of us helping in catching lizards in the school for the whole term!"

The whole room burst with laughter upon hearing this.

Satpal joined in, "Those were some tough times. But we learned our lesson, and Tapinder, especially, became more disciplined. We became famously called the dino catchers since lizards are considered descendants of dinosaurs".

The trio laughed, sharing stories highlighting Tapinder's naughty side and Joginder Singh's firm but fair parenting style.

As the family settled down, stories of Tapinder's childhood flowed freely. Laughter filled the air as they shared anecdotes of his pranks, his dreams, and the bond that had bound the brothers together.

Tracy and Sarah listened with rapt attention, feeling connected to the man they had lost.

Tracy and Sarah found themselves enveloped in the warmth of this extended family, a family they had never known but who welcomed them with open hearts.

Amid the laughter, Satpal raised an empty glass. "To new beginnings and cherished memories. To Tapinder's legacy and the bonds that unite us."

The clinking of glasses resonated, weaving seamlessly into a night adorned with tales of tempting delicacies, the warmth of shared laughter, and a flickering bonfire casting dancing shadows in the heart of the courtyard, embracing the cold night in its comforting glow.

Perplexed by the overly warm reception from the family, Sarah sought clarification from Tracy. "Tracy, isn't their hospitality a bit overwhelming, considering they haven't even met or spoken to us, especially when their son severed ties because of you?"

Tracy silently nodded and softly spoke, "It truly reflects this family's love for Tapinder. Cutting ties must have been a painful decision for them, and I can't help but feel guilty about it."

Overhearing Tracy's words, Joginder Singh Ji said, "Tracy, it's not your fault. Perhaps Tapinder and my ego got the best of us. In fact, we owe you an apology for not welcoming you into our family sooner."

Touched by Joginder Singh Ji's sincere words, Tracy and Sarah exchanged heartfelt glances.

On the room's periphery, Rekha and Tannu, Joginder Singh Ji's daughters-in-law, appeared uneasy, seemingly not favouring Tracy and Sarah's presence.

Later in the night, the family gathered in a circle under the starlit sky. Satpal Singh's voice carried a mixture of nostalgia and determination as he spoke. "Tomorrow, let's gather at Bholaghat – the place where Tapinder, Kripashankar, and I used to play as children. It's by the banks of the river Ganga, a place where our memories reside. We'll immerse Tapinder's ashes there, and he'll become a part of the land he loved."

Tears welled up in Sarah's eyes as she looked around at the faces of Tapinder's family. Tracy's hand found hers, offering silent comfort. Sarah's voice was filled with gratitude and a sense of belonging. "Thank you, all, for letting us participate in this journey. For giving us a chance to connect with Tapinder's roots."

Joginder Singh's hand rested on Sarah's shoulder, his gaze gentle yet steadfast. "Family is not just about blood, Sarah. It's about the bonds we forge and the memories we share. Tomorrow, we'll gather as a family – to celebrate Tapinder's life and to find closure."

As the night deepened, the family bid each other goodnight, the fire's embers glowing softly in the darkness. Sarah and Tracy retired to their room, their hearts full of emotions they had never expected to feel in a place so far from home.

Underneath the starry sky, the village lay still, a testament to the enduring power of family and the journey of healing that had only just begun. And as the night whispered its secrets, the promise of a new day brought the hope of finding closure, discovering a sense of belonging, and honouring the legacy of a beloved father and son.

CHAPTER 9

Immersing the Ashes

The morning sun painted the sky with shades of pink and gold as Majid drove the family towards the banks of the river. The car bumped along the narrow village roads, the tyres stirring up dust. Inside the vehicle, the atmosphere was a mix of solemnity and anticipation.

Next to Majid sat Joginder Singh, his weathered face a canvas of emotions. In the backseat, Tracy sat, her gaze fixed on the earthen pot containing Tapinder's ashes. Her heart was heavy with the moment's weight, the significance of bidding a final farewell to the man she had loved. Beside her were Rekha and Tannu, her sisters-in-law, who held a tension in their posture that went beyond the sad occasion.

As the car neared the river, the sound of flowing water became more pronounced. Majid guided the vehicle to a stop. The air was still, and the reverence matched the occasion.

Amid this solemn scene, tension simmered within the car. Rekha and Tannu exchanged glances, their expressions guarded. They had not been particularly welcoming to Tracy and Sarah's presence, harbouring their concerns and insecurities.

Rekha's voice broke the silence, laced with a hint of bitterness. "Tracy, this is a celebratory time for the family. We appreciate your presence here, but once the rituals are done, it might be best for you and Sarah to return to America."

Tannu nodded in agreement, her eyes avoiding Tracy's gaze. "Yes, that's what Tapinder always wanted. He left his family for the comfort of America and never turned back. The town will question you and Sarah staying with us, which can create problems for our daughter Neetu's wedding."

Tracy's heart sank as the weight of their words settled in. She understood their concerns. But it was a bitter pill, especially in this vulnerability and grief.

Joginder Singh's eyes narrowed as he overheard the conversation, his voice firm as he addressed his daughters-in-law. "Rekha, Tannu, we are a family united by love and loss. Let us not taint this moment with doubts and suspicions. Tapinder chose his own path, and so did Sarah and Tracy. They are a part of our family, and their presence does not need approval from anyone."

Tracy felt gratitude for Joginder Singh Ji's support. She felt a renewed sense of belonging, a validation of the bond she had forged with Tapinder's family.

Sarah arrived with her cousins Vicky, Jolly, and Neetu. The atmosphere was sombre yet filled with a sense of purpose. As they stepped out of the car, Vicky, a young man with a cheerful demeanour, grinned at Sarah. "Hey, cousin! Long time no see. How's life in New York treating you?"

Sarah returned the smile. "It's been busy but good. Working at the family business and all."

Jolly chimed in with a playful tone. "So, you're trying to be the #1 Retail store chain in the US, huh? I read about your business on a few news websites."

Sarah chuckled, glancing at Neetu, the youngest of the trio, who was busy capturing the serene landscape with her phone. "Well, we are doing our best. But how's life here in India?"

Neetu finally looked up, a mischievous twinkle in her eyes. "Oh, you know, the usual chaos, traffic jams, and endless family gatherings."

Sarah laughed, feeling the familiar bond with her cousins. "It sounds like India, alright. But you guys have a front-row seat to all the changes happening here."

Vicky nodded, his expression turning more serious. "Absolutely. India's becoming a superpower in various sectors, and everyone's looking to invest here. It's an exciting time."

Jolly added, "Yeah, the world's recognising India's potential in technology, manufacturing, and more."

Neetu chimed in with enthusiasm. "And you know what's the best part? We, the youth, are driving this change. We're the ones shaping the future. Hence, we never considered leaving our country and settling in Western countries."

Sarah's eyes sparkled with pride as she listened to her cousins. "You're right. It's amazing to see how far India has come. And it makes me feel even more connected to my roots."

As they walked towards the riverbank, Sarah looked around at the lush greenery and the tranquil water.

Neetu tapped Sarah's shoulder and said, "This place holds so many memories for our family. It's where our fathers used to play when they were kids."

Vicky nodded, his voice tinged with nostalgia. "I remember hearing stories from Dad about their adventures here."

In his serious tone, Jolly said, "Sarah, you might have lost your father, but his legacy lives on. And now, you're here to carry that legacy forward."

Sarah smiled warmly at her cousins, touched by their words. "Thank you, guys. It means a lot to me."

Joginder Singh and his sons Kripashankar and Satpal approached the water's edge, their steps slow and measured. The earthen pot cradled in their hands held the last remains of Tapinder. Tracy and Sarah stood beside them, a silent support amidst the vastness of their emotions. The others gathered around, their expressions a mixture of sadness and reflection.

As Joginder Singh Ji lowered the pot into the water, a peaceful silence enveloped the group. The river's surface rippled gently, carrying away the ashes and the memories they held. The moment was a testament to the circle of life – the cycle of birth, growth, and eventual return to the earth.

As the ashes dissolved into the river's current, so did the tension that had hung in the air. The family stood in quiet reflection, the river's gentle flow a reminder of the passage of time.

As the sun climbed higher in the sky, casting a warm glow over the water, a sense of peace settled the group. They were bound not just by blood but by shared memories, the legacy of a beloved son and brother, and the understanding that love and unity could triumph over all challenges.

The cousins, including Sarah, exchanged glances, understanding the moment's significance. Together, they held hands as they walked away from the river, slowly looking away from the water's gentle current.

As the sun illuminated the water's surface, Sarah felt a renewed sense of purpose, a determination to carry forward her father's dreams, and a bond with her family that transcended time and distance.

CHAPTER 10

Sisters-in-law

In the dimly lit corners of the Singh household, Rekha and Tannu, the orchestrators of chaos, huddled together to discuss eliminating the foreigners. The room echoed with whispered conspiracies as they tried to salvage what was left of their ill-conceived plot.

With a scowl, Rekha muttered, "I can't believe Sasurji (Joginder Singh) is allowing Tracy and Sarah to stay in the house and attend the wedding."

Tannu, equally displeased, responded, "We should've been more careful yesterday when speaking to Tracy, but we can't let this opportunity slip away. We need to get rid of Tracy and Sarah before the wedding."

The duo began to strategise their next move. "Let's make it more personal this time," Rekha suggested with a sinister glint in her eyes. We'll target Joginder Singh's prized possession—his vintage car. A punctured tyre will surely create a commotion."

Tannu nodded in agreement. "And let's remember the cow. We'll 'lose' it this time. That beast is causing too much trouble anyway."

As they delved deeper into their conniving plans, the two women contemplated other ways to disrupt the peace in the household. Rekha proposed, "What if local goons attack the foreigners? They will surely run away."

Tannu asked surprisingly, "From where will you get these goons?"

Rekha responded, "My brother has helped hire these goons, and they are going to attack tonight to scare the foreign women."

Tannu smirked, pleased with the suggestion. "Perfect. Joginder Singh can't do anything in this case."

Little did they know that Neetu, who had been eavesdropping outside the door, had overheard their conversation. Concerned for the family's unity, she decided to take matters into her own hands.

As the tension in the Singh household escalated, hidden agendas and thwarted plans threatened to unravel the familial fabric. Neetu, torn between loyalty to her family and a sense of justice, grappled with the impending storm.

The night draped the Singh household in an uneasy quiet, broken only by the distant howls of the wind. In the dimly lit corridors, Neetu discreetly approached Tracy and Sarah, her eyes brimming with worry. She whispered, "Aunt Rekha and Mom are planning something against you both. It's not safe for you here."

Tracy and Sarah exchanged concerned glances. Tracy whispered back, "We need to leave, Sarah. It's not safe."

Sarah, though hesitant, nodded in agreement. Sensing the impending danger, they decided it was best to leave. In the tranquil hours of the night, guided by Majid, they gathered their belongings and headed towards the door, planning to retreat to a hotel in Dehradun.

However, as they stepped into the night, their departure coincided with an unforeseen twist. In the shadows, a group of intruders hired by the sisters-in-law slipped through the back door to attack Sarah and Tracy.

The dogs outside the home, guardians of the night, sensed the intrusion and erupted into furious barking, alerting the entire household. Panic seized the would-be thieves, who quickly entered the verandah brandishing knives.

In a twist of fate, the intruders saw the valuable ornaments Rekha and Tannu were wearing and attacked them instead.

The chaotic commotion brought the entire household to a startled awakening.

Rekha and Tannu were terror-struck. Rekha, pleading with the intruders, said, "We hired you to scare the foreigners, but you are attacking us instead."

The thieves, cornered and desperate, seized Rekha and Tannu, holding them at knifepoint in the veranda's middle. Their threats echoed through the night, demanding silence or risking the lives of the hostages.

It was a moment of sheer terror until, in an unexpected turn, Tracy and Sarah leapt into action, armed with their knowledge of self-defence. With a flurry of flying kicks, they overpowered the goons, driving them back and freeing Rekha and Tannu.

The drama unfolded in seconds, leaving the goons scrambling. Fearing further confrontation, they fled into the night, leaving behind the chaos they had instigated.

Rekha and Tannu, once adversaries, now stood in awe of the courage displayed by Tracy and Sarah.

As the night's chaos slowly subsided, Tracy and Sarah stood amidst the shaken Singh household. Rekha and Tannu, their faces now etched with fear and remorse, approached the two women.

Rekha hesitated momentarily before speaking, "Tracy, Sarah, we... we're sorry.

We never thought... we didn't expect this to happen."

Tannu nodded. "We are sorry. Please stay. We need you here for the wedding. We promise we won't cause any more trouble."

Echoing her sentiments, Rekha said, "Your presence saved us tonight. We owe you, and we're grateful. Please stay."

The night had brought about an unexpected turn of events, softening the hearts that were once rigid with animosity. The exchange, though brief, carried the weight of reconciliation, and the air slowly shifted from tension to a fragile truce.

In the aftermath of the night's chaos, Majid, Vicky, Neetu, and Jolly were happy with the unexpected twist. The family is brought to the brink of disintegration, and they find an unlikely glue in Tracy and Sarah's bravery.

CHAPTER 11

Going around Behalpur

The crisp morning air greeted Sarah and Tracy as they embarked on an impromptu adventure around the charming town of Behalpur. The cobblestone streets echoed with the rhythmic pattern of their running shoes as they weaved through little quaint homes, each holding its own piece of the town's history.

With the rising sun casting a golden glow on the distant mountains, the duo couldn't resist the allure of the rugged trails that led upwards. Their breaths mingled with the mountain breeze as they ascended, the panoramic views unfolding with every step.

As Sarah and Tracy reached the mountaintop, a serene silence enveloped them, broken only by the distant echoes of birdsong and the gentle rustling of leaves. The panoramic view stretched before them, the town of Behalpur nestled like a story in the embrace of the mountains.

Sarah, catching her breath, looked out over the landscape. "Tracy, can you believe we're here? It's like stepping into a painting."

Her eyes reflecting the moment's awe, Tracy replied, "Absolutely, Sarah. This place is magical. I can see why Tapinder loved it so much. But I wonder why he never came back."

Sarah nodded thoughtfully. "You know, Tracy, life in Behalpur seems so different from the hustle and bustle of New York. It's like time slows down here."

Scanning the horizon, Tracy added, "And yet, there's a timeless beauty to it. I feel like we're part of something bigger, something rooted in history."

As they sat on a rocky outcrop, the town below now a miniature world, Sarah asked, "What do you think Tapinder found in New York that he couldn't find here?"

Looking into the distance, Tracy mused, "Maybe a sense of belonging. It's a different pace of life, and I guess he found solace in the hustle and bustle of creating a business in America and generating employment for people like him away from home."

Sarah nodded a wistful smile on her lips. "You're right. But sometimes, we get so caught up in the chase for success that we forget to appreciate the moments. I wish I had the chance to experience these moments with Dad."

With a thoughtful expression, Tracy said, "Maybe that's what we can take back. The reminder to savour life, whether in the quiet charm of Behalpur or the bustling streets of New York."

As they descended the mountain, the conversation continued, weaving through family topics, the contrast of two worlds, and the realisation that sometimes, the most profound discoveries are made in the quiet corners of the heart.

Majid, ever the courteous guide, joined them on their descent. The car ride back to the heart of Behalpur was filled with shared laughter and tales of the town's hidden gems. With a twinkle in his eye, Majid recounted anecdotes about the ancient structures and the stories etched in the very fabric of Behalpur.

As they meandered through the narrow lanes, Majid pointed out landmarks and shared snippets of local folklore, turning the journey back into a captivating exploration.

Majid, Tracy, and Sarah engaged in a delightful exchange of stories as they journeyed through the winding lanes of Behalpur. The car's wheels hummed a rhythmic tune against the cobblestone streets, setting the backdrop for their lively conversation.

His eyes reflecting his pride for his town, Majid began, "You see that ancient banyan tree over there? Legend has it that it's as old as time itself. Locals believe it's a keeper of secrets, a silent witness to the town's evolution."

Tracy, intrigued, leaned forward. "Really? That's fascinating. I love how every corner here seems to have a story."

Majid chuckled, "Oh, you haven't heard the half of it. Behalpur has tales woven into its very bricks. Take that old haveli, for instance. It once housed a reclusive poet who penned verses that still echo in the quiet alleys."

Captivated by the narratives, Sarah said, "It's like every stone has a story to tell."

Majid nodded, "Exactly. You two are not just visiting Behalpur; you're becoming part of its story. Now, speaking of stories, wait till I tell you about the mysterious well at the edge of town."

Tracy grinned, "Mysterious, well? Count me in. What's the story behind it?"

Adopting a mysterious tone, Majid began, "Legend has it that the water from that well has magical properties. Couples who drink from it are said to have everlasting love."

With a playful smile, Tracy teased, "Well then, we can't miss that well, can we, Sarah?"

Sarah laughed, "Absolutely not. I could use some everlasting love in my life."

The trio continued their banter, blending historical anecdotes with their lighthearted tales. Behalpur, with its charm and stories, became more than a town; it became a shared experience, a journey etched in laughter and camaraderie.

As they strolled through Behalpur, Majid guided Sarah and Tracy to a quaint spot behind the town's bustling market—a small pond surrounded by lush greenery. The sunlight danced on the water's surface, casting a mesmerising glow.

Majid, with a mischievous smile, pointed to the pond. "Behold, the Wishing Pond. They say your wish comes true if you drop a Rs.10 coin in there."

Sarah raised an eyebrow, sceptical. "Really? Sounds like a good way to make some money for those boys diving in for the coins."

Majid chuckled, "Ah, you've seen those documentaries, haven't you? Well, I won't deny some boys retrieve the coins later. But the wishes, Sarah, they do come true."

Sarah sarcastically remarked, "Why doesn't the pond have a QR code for one to pay Rs.10 digitally?"

Intrigued, Tracy nudged Sarah, "Come on, let's try it. What's the harm in making a little wish?"

With a twinkle in his eye, Majid produced a Rs. 10 coin. "Here you go, Sarah. Give it a shot."

Sarah, still doubtful but playing along, took the coin. With a theatrical flourish, she tossed it into the pond. The ripples spread, reflecting the sunlight like a thousand diamonds.

Closing her eyes, Sarah made her wish silently. Majid and Tracy exchanged amused glances.

Tracy teased, "So, what's the secret wish, Sarah? World peace, a million dollars, or maybe an endless supply of mangoes?"

With a mysterious smile, Sarah replied, "You'll know when the time comes."

As they continued exploring Behalpur, the Wishing Pond became a whimsical memory, blending scepticism and hope. And who knows, perhaps somewhere in the depths of that pond, Sarah's wish was waiting to unfurl with time.

CHAPTER 12

Buying the Perfect Lehenga

The morning sun painted Behalpur in warm hues as Tracy and Sarah returned to Joginder Singh Ji and Amarjeet Kaur's home. The aroma of brewing tea welcomed them even before they entered.

Sitting on the porch, Joginder Singh Ji looked up with a wide smile. "Ah, the early birds return. How was your morning run, my dears?"

With a grin, Tracy replied, "Refreshing, Joginder Singh Ji. Your town is truly a gem."

Amarjeet Kaur, emerging from the kitchen with a tray of steaming tea, added, "I'm delighted to see you two exploring Behalpur. It warms my heart."

They settled on the porch, the cups of tea warming their hands. Joginder Singh Ji observed, "So, any exciting discoveries on your morning adventure?"

Sarah animatedly shared the story of the Wishing Pond: "If you drop a Rs. 10 coin, your wish comes true. We were a bit sceptical, but we gave it a try."

Joginder Singh Ji chuckled. "Ah, the Wishing Pond. Many stories and wishes must have been shared there over the years."

Tracy, sipping her tea, added, "It's a charming tradition. Majid says some boys dive in later to collect the coins."

Joginder Singh Ji nodded. "Yes, the boys do that, but the wishes, my dear, they have a way of finding their path."

As the conversation flowed, Amarjeet Kaur joined in. "You know, Tracy, Sarah, we were thinking about Neetu's wedding. We hope you both can wear a traditional lehenga for the occasion. In Delhi, you'll find the finest choices. Could you do us the favour of selecting one for yourself? And the lehengas are on us as a gift from our side."

Tracy and Sarah exchanged glances, happy to be part of the wedding preparations. "Of course, Amarjeet Kaur. We'd be honoured," Tracy replied.

With a twinkle in his eye, Joginder Singh Ji said, "Excellent. Neetu, Vicky and Jolly are travelling to Chandni Chowk today. Why don't you both join them?

The Singh youngsters, including Tracy and Sarah, embarked on a bustling adventure to Delhi. The air was thick with excitement as they delved into the vibrant chaos of one of Delhi's oldest markets.

Neetu took the wheel, her eyes sparkling with the excitement of finding the ideal lehenga. Racing the highway, she glanced at Sarah seated beside her in the front. She exclaimed, "Badal Arora Ji, Dadaji's longtime friend and a renowned designer in the heart of Chandni Chowk, has promised some truly exquisite creations for you and Tracy."

Sarah admired Neetu's driving skills and commented, "Everyone here is a car enthusiast. Speaking of cars, Jolly, when is that infamous mountain race everyone talks about? The one they say is quite risky." Jolly grinned, "It's happening a day right after Neetu's wedding."

Sarah inquired, "How's your practice going? Do you think you'll finally outpace Ravi Chandar this time?"

Jolly, taken aback, queried, "How do you even know about Ravi Chandar? Let me guess: Majid spilled the beans. Ravi's been the reigning champion for three years, but my gut says he's meeting his match this time."

Vicky, intrigued, interjected, "Jolly, what makes you so sure?"

Brimming with confidence, Jolly explained, "I've been putting in serious practice hours this year, hitting high speeds with remarkable stability. Ask Majid if you doubt me."

Neetu teased, "Just a week away from the race, and you're here enjoying Delhi with us, convinced you can beat the phantom of Behalpur!"

Laughter erupted among the group.

Neetu quickly drove as she navigated the bylanes and stopped the car outside the Arora & Sons store.

As they entered the store, fabrics in myriad hues dazzled under the bright lights.

With a twinkle in her eye, Neetu headed straight to the turquoise lehenga she had chosen for her engagement. The intricate embroidery and delicate sequins sparkled, and Neetu couldn't hide her joy. "Isn't it stunning?" she beamed, twirling in front of the mirror.

Sarah and Tracy were equally enchanted. "Absolutely breathtaking!" Tracy exclaimed, her eyes wide with admiration. Sarah nodded in agreement, "Neetu, you'll be the most beautiful bride."

The next revelation brought a new wave of excitement. Badal, the designer, turned to Tracy and Sarah, "And for our lovely guests, we have something special." He revealed a collection of vibrant lehenga cholis, each more splendid than the last.

Although unfamiliar with the intricate details, Tracy couldn't help but feel a sense of belonging as she slipped into the traditional attire. "I never thought I'd wear something like this," she admitted, smiling.

Sarah, fully embracing the vibrant colours, twirled in front of the mirror. "Tapinder always wanted me to try Indian Lehenga Dresses. I guess this is my chance."

The vibrant fabrics of the lehengas shimmered under the boutique lights as Sarah sifted through the dazzling collection. Neetu, Jolly, and Vicky gathered, eager to witness the transformation.

With a mischievous glint in her eye, Neetu teased, "Sarah, you're already turning heads, and the wedding hasn't even started. Wait until you step out in one of those lehengas. You'll have a line of suitors by the night's end!"

Jolly, playing along, added, "I can already hear the wedding bells ringing. Who knew all it took was a stunning lehenga to attract the perfect match?"

Vicky quipped, "Watch out, Sarah. You might need security cover to handle the flood of proposals."

Blushing at the playful banter, Sarah laughed, "Oh, please! It's just a dress."

Tracy, admiring her daughter's beauty, chimed in, "No, Sarah, it's not just a dress. It's a piece of art, and you look absolutely breathtaking."

Neetu, picking out another lehenga, held it up. "Let's try this one. Who knows, maybe this will be the showstopper at the wedding!"

As Sarah stepped into the next lehenga, the cousins continued their playful commentary, creating an atmosphere of joy and excitement in the boutique. The dazzling colours and intricate designs added to the festive spirit, and everyone eagerly anticipated the grand reveal of each new ensemble.

After a few hours, the Singh family emerged from the store, laden with a trove of shopping bags, creating a colourful cascade that found its place in the awaiting car.

The Singh family's shopping escapade continued as they explored the bylanes of Chandni Chowk. Amidst the sea of fabrics and bustling shoppers, they stumbled upon a famous paratha joint. The aroma of sizzling parathas wafted through the air, and the family couldn't resist indulging in the delectable delights.

With a mischievous grin, Tracy teased Sarah, "I hope these parathas are as good as the stories Tapinder used to tell us about the Delhi street food."

Sarah chuckled, savouring the first bite, "I have to admit, they live up to the hype."

The aroma of freshly cooked parathas wafted through the air as Vicky, Jolly, Neetu, Tracy, and Sarah gathered around the dining table. The table was laden with various parathas—stuffed with potatoes, paneer, and spices. A friendly competition was about to unfold.

Vicky, known for his voracious appetite, threw down the gauntlet. "Let's see who can devour the most parathas! The winner gets a treat from everyone else."

Jolly, always up for a challenge, grinned. "You're on, Vicky. But remember, I have the appetite of a lion."

Neetu, competitive as ever, said, "I won't lose to my brothers. Get ready, Tracy and Sarah; this is a Singh family paratha showdown!"

Tracy, up for the fun, winked at Sarah. "I hope they have a separate category for the fastest eater. I might give these boys a run for their money."

The paratha feast began. Plates were stacked with the flaky, golden-brown delights. Laughter echoed between bites as they raced to finish one paratha after another. The competition grew intense, with each participant determined to outdo the others.

As the paratha count rose, Vicky emerged as the undisputed champion. With a triumphant grin, he declared, "Looks like Vicky Singh reigns supreme in paratha eating."

Cheers erupted, and everyone congratulated Vicky on his impressive feat. In the spirit of good sportsmanship, they decided to treat Vicky to his favourite halwa from a popular store in Karol Bagh.

The group headed out, still full from the paratha challenge but eager for the next culinary adventure. The streets of Delhi embraced them as they made their way to the sweet shop, their laughter blending with the vibrant rhythm of the city.

As they strolled through Delhi, laden with shopping bags and hearts full of warmth, Tracy, Sarah, and the Singh family forged bonds that cut through cultural differences. In the spirit of Delhi's chaos, a beautiful symphony of traditions, laughter, and the promise of new beginnings played out, leaving everyone eager for the grand celebration that awaited them.

CHAPTER 13

Planning the Bachelorette

The sun dipped below the horizon, casting a warm glow on Behalpur as Tracy and Sarah huddled together, conspiring with excitement.

"You know, Sarah, we should totally throw a bachelorette party for Neetu! It'll be a blast," Tracy exclaimed, her eyes gleaming with mischievous delight.

Sarah enthusiastically nodded, "Absolutely! We can have games and music and maybe even hire a dancer. Neetu will love it!"

As they were deep in planning, Vicky, Jolly, and Neetu approached, exchanging secretive glances. Vicky winked at Jolly, "Looks like they're up to something."

Neetu tried to suppress a grin, "Well, we've got something special in mind, too. Just you wait."

Tracy raised an eyebrow, "Oh, really? What's your big plan?"

Jolly chuckled, "It's a surprise, but we promise it'll be unforgettable."

Sarah looked at Neetu, "You sly little thing! You knew we were planning something."

Neetu laughed, "Guilty as charged. But hey, the more, the merrier, right? Let's combine our efforts and make it the best bachelorette party ever!"

Tracy agreed, "True! The more ideas, the better. Let's coordinate and make Neetu's night unforgettable."

So, the cousins merged their plans, crafting a bachelorette extravaganza that would become the stuff of legends in Behalpur. Little did they know they were in for a night filled with surprises and joy, courtesy of her mischievous but loving cousins.

As the excitement for Neetu's bachelorette party continued to build, the lively discussion shifted to the choice of venue. Vicky and Jolly, with mischievous grins, declared, "We've booked a fantastic farmhouse in Dehradun for the ultimate party experience."

Neetu's eyes lit up, "Dehradun? That sounds amazing!"

Vicky nodded, "Absolutely! Now, for the theme – it will be a dance competition!"

Jolly added, "That's right. We'll have two teams, but don't worry, Neetu, you, Tracy, and Sarah are all on the same team. We're just adding a fun twist."

Neetu laughed, "Phew, I thought you were separating us. What's the twist?"

Vicky winked, "Ah, that's a secret for now. But trust us, it'll be a riot!"

Jolly said, "Now, onto the most crucial aspect – food! Only biryani and kebabs are on the menu."

Neetu teased, "Are you trying to make us sleep after party?"

Vicky grinned, "Maybe just a little."

Sarah, ever the music enthusiast, jumped in, "Well, speaking of dancing, I'm taking over as the DJ. Get ready for some killer tunes, folks!"

And so, the plans for Neetu's bachelorette party evolved, promising an unforgettable night filled with laughter, friendly competition, and a few surprises up their sleeves.

The cousins, somewhat sceptical about Sarah's DJ skills, couldn't hide their surprise when she confidently declared, "No worries, guys! I've got an awesome collection of Hindi, Punjabi, and Bollywood tracks. I used to DJ for my friends back in New Jersey, and they loved it!"

Vicky, Jolly, and Neetu exchanged astonished glances. "Really? You DJ in New Jersey?" Vicky asked, raising an eyebrow.

Sarah grinned, "Oh, yes! I know exactly what music will get everyone on the dance floor. Bollywood, Punjabi, and Bhangra – you name it, I've got it."

Jolly, impressed, chimed in, "That's perfect! We don't want any of that Western stuff. We need good, foot-tapping beats that we can dance to."

Proud of her daughter's unexpected talent, Tracy added, "You're in for a treat, then. Sarah knows how to keep a party alive with her music choices."

As the cousins envisioned a night filled with energetic desi beats, they began to appreciate the unique and diverse skills each family member was bringing to Neetu's bachelorette party. The anticipation for the celebration continued to grow.

With a mischievous glint in his eyes, Vicky leaned in to share his part of the plan. "Don't worry, guys! I've got the booze covered. It'll be delivered directly to the farmhouse."

Jolly, always enthusiastic about his contributions, jumped in, "And guess what? Majid taking care of the lights. I've got this awesome LED setup that will turn the farmhouse into a party haven. Majid is going to set it up for us."

Majid, who had been listening quietly, nodded in agreement. "Absolutely. I've got the setup covered. We'll transform that farmhouse into the ultimate party zone."

The cousins exchanged impressed looks. "You guys are killing it with the planning," Neetu exclaimed. The excitement for the pre-wedding party was building up, and the anticipation for the celebration reached new heights with each passing moment.

Tracy, with a raised eyebrow, interrupted the lively conversation. "Hold on, boys! Isn't a bachelorette supposed to be a girls' night out? Why are we involving the whole jing-bang?"

Neetu, the bride-to-be, grinned mischievously. "Tracy, it's a pre-party to the wedding in the true sense. We want everyone to let loose before the big day."

Tracy pondered momentarily, thinking about her comfort level at a party filled with youngsters. "I don't know, Neetu. I feel a bit out of place in these kinds of gatherings."

Vicky chimed in, "Come on, Tracy! It's going to be epic. You can't miss out on the Fun."

Neetu added, "And you know how our families are. If only youngsters were at the party, the elders would raise eyebrows. Having you around will be the perfect cover."

Tracy sighed, realising the practicality of the situation. "Fine, but I'm not promising to keep up with you young folks."

The cousins cheered, thrilled that Tracy had agreed to participate in the festivities.

CHAPTER 14

Preparing for the Events

With just 8 days to go for the wedding festivities, Joginder Singh Ji, the patriarch of the Singh family, stood at the centre of the room, his eyes reflecting the wisdom of years. "Now, let me outline the sequence of events for Neetu's wedding celebrations," he began, his voice carrying the weight of tradition and the joy of upcoming festivities.

"On the 10th of December, we kick off the celebrations with the Sangeet. Vicky and Jolly, I want this night filled with music, dance, and laughter. It's a time for our families and friends to come together and celebrate the union of two families."

"Two days later, on the 12th of December, we have the Engagement ceremony. Neetu, this is your responsibility. It's your moment to exchange rings, marking the beginning of a beautiful journey. Please check with the decorator to see when we can see the setup."

"The most auspicious day, the 14th of December, is reserved for the wedding. Majid, as I mentioned earlier, you will oversee this grand event. It's the heart of the celebrations, a day when traditions will be honoured, and two souls will unite. Please tell the decorator about the arrangements and remind him about the grandeur look we want. No artificial flowers will be used. I want everything natural. Also, are we going to get to taste the food?"

Joginder Singh Ji's eyes twinkled as he continued, "And finally, on the 16th of December, we'll have a post-wedding party. Jolly, you know the drill, right? Music, Food, Drinks?"

The room absorbed the significance of each event, and the family members nodded in agreement. The calendar of celebrations was set, promising a week filled with love, tradition, and the joyous union of two souls.

Joginder Singh Ji, a man deeply involved in the intricacies of traditional family celebrations, now moved his attention to the upcoming mountain car race.

He sat down with Jolly and Majid to discuss the race. They gathered in the garage filled with charts, diagrams, and the smell of engine oil. This space bore witness to the fusion of tradition and modernity.

Joginder Singh Ji, leaning forward, asked, "Jolly, how are the race preparations coming along?"

Jolly, the spirited racer, shared the details of their modifications to the car. "Majid and I have been working on tuning up the engine. We've been focusing on the power-to-weight ratio, considering the importance of rapid acceleration and responsive throttle performance in the race."

Joginder Singh Ji, always keen on details, nodded. "Power-to-weight ratio is crucial. What are you doing to enhance it?"

Majid, the skilled mechanic and racing enthusiast, chimed in. "We're using lightweight materials like aluminium alloys for the cylinder heads to keep the engine weight as low as possible. Additionally, we're exploring forced induction through supercharging to increase power without significantly adding to the engine's weight."

Joginder's eyes gleamed with anticipation. "Good choices. What about the bore size to piston stroke ratio?"

Majid explained, "For a high-power output engine, like the one needed for a sports car, an over-square configuration with a shorter piston stroke is favourable. This allows for higher engine speeds and better breathing at high RPMs."

Joginder nodded approvingly. "And what about the centre of gravity? It's crucial for handling, especially in the tricky hilly areas."

Majid continued, "We're aiming for a low centre of gravity. The boxer engine layout, with horizontally opposed cylinders, helps achieve this. It minimises weight transfer during cornering in steep mountain hairpin bends, contributing to better handling and control."

Joginder Singh Ji scrutinised Jolly, his eyes keen with the expectation of thorough preparation. "Jolly, how much practice have you had with the upgraded car in the mountains?"

A bit sheepish, Jolly responded, "Dadaji, I've been caught up with the wedding preparations, and I must admit, the practice has taken a backseat. But, with the race just around the corner, I'm gearing up to give it my all."

Majid, the ever-supportive ally in Jolly's racing endeavours, said, "Dadaji, Jolly has a great chance this year. The upgrades we've made to the car and his driving skills can make a significant difference."

Joginder, though concerned about the limited practice, nodded in understanding. "Weddings demand attention, but the race is also crucial. Ensure you spend enough time practising in the mountains in the coming days. It's a different beast altogether, and familiarity is key."

Inspired by the support, Jolly assured them, "Absolutely, Dadaji. I'll make the most of the days left. Majid and I will fine-tune everything, and you'll see the best performance from our side."

Joginder, acknowledging the commitment, smiled. "Good. A Singh doesn't back away from challenges. This year, let the mountains echo with the roar of our victory. I have faith in you, Jolly."

With a discerning gaze, Joginder Singh Ji inquired about Jolly and Majid's reconnaissance on Ravi Chandar's car upgrades. "Have you looked into what Ravi is doing with his car? You know he has the means to import high-end parts from countries like Japan and Germany."

Following the competition, Majid responded, "Yes, Dadaji. We've done our research. Ravi is indeed investing heavily in top-notch upgrades. His car is likely to be formidable, much like ours."

With determination, Jolly added, "But we're not lagging behind. The upgrades we've chosen are on par with the best. While Ravi might have the resources, we have the skill and a deep understanding of these mountains. We're ready to give him a run for his money this year."

Joginder nodded approvingly. "Good. It's not just about the car; it's about the synergy between man and machine. The mountains favour those who understand them. Keep a close eye on Ravi's progress, and ensure our car is finely tuned for the race. We're not just competing; we're aiming for victory."

With a twinkle in his eye, Joginder Singh Ji looked at Jolly and Majid. "Let's see this marvel you've been working on. Bring the car out."

Jolly revved the engine with pride, and the sleek yellow sports car emerged from the garage, its roar echoing through the mountain air. Audited by the transformation, Tracy and Sarah joined Joginder Singh Ji as they approached the car.

Joginder opened the door, gesturing for Tracy and Sarah to join him. "Come, let's take this beauty for a spin in the mountains. I want you to experience the thrill of these winding roads."

Tracy and Sarah excitedly took their seats, feeling the hum of the powerful engine beneath them. The car smoothly navigated the hilly terrain as Joginder expertly manoeuvred through the curves. The wind whistled through the open windows, and the breathtaking scenery unfolded before them.

As they ascended higher, Joginder turned to Tracy and Sarah and said, "Hold tight, ladies. This is where the real Fun begins."

The car zipped through the mountain roads, the acceleration and deceleration perfectly synchronised with the twists and turns. Caught in the exhilarating moment,

Tracy and Sarah couldn't help but laugh and cheer. The mountain breeze played with their hair as they enjoyed the adrenaline-pumping ride.

Joginder Singh Ji, with a grin, glanced at them. "Feeling the rush, aren't you?"

Her eyes gleamed; Tracy replied, "This is incredible, Joginder Singh Ji! You've got a real gem here."

The car's growl softened as they descended to the Singh residence. Tracy and Sarah, still buzzing with excitement, stepped out, thanking Joginder for the unforgettable ride. The sports car, now parked in its spot, radiates the energy of the mountain adventure, setting the stage for the upcoming race.

As they discussed the upcoming practice sessions and finalised the last-minute adjustments, the anticipation for the race hung in the air. The melding of family responsibilities with the pursuit of victory created a unique blend, echoing the Singh family's unwavering spirit.

Joginder Singh Ji leaned back, satisfied with the technical insights. "Keep pushing the boundaries, Jolly. Let's aim to beat Ravi Chandar this year and set a new record. The family is counting on you."

Jolly, filled with determination, replied, "We'll give it our all, Dadaji. Majid and I are committed to making this race one for the books."

Tracy said, "Joginder Singh Ji, how did the flame of racing passion begin?"

"It all started with Majid's father," Joginder began, a nostalgic glint in his eyes. "He was not just an auto mechanic; he was an artist with engines.

Back in those days, our love for racing was just budding. I used to bring my car to Majid's father for repairs, and he saw something in me – a desire for speed."

Sitting with a modest smile, Majid listened as Joginder Singh Ji continued the story. "He suggested I try racing and tune up my old car for the first race. I'll never forget that day – the rush, the competition. It was like discovering a part of myself I never knew existed."

Joginder Singh Ji's gaze shifted to Majid. "Your father was a mentor, Majid, a guide who fueled my passion. He believed in speed, precision, and the art of racing. With every race, I learned and grew. And now, seeing that tradition carried on by Majid is heartening."

He turned to Majid, "You've maintained and elevated the legacy. Your expertise, dedication, and love for the craft have made us formidable contenders. The next generation races because you continue to provide the wisdom your father once imparted to me."

Majid, humbled by Joginder Singh Ji's words, nodded. "It's an honour to contribute to this legacy, to be part of something deeper than just the thrill of speed. Racing, for us, is a connection – to the past, to the essence of our town, and to the spirit that drives us forward."

Theatrically, Neetu suddenly burst into the ongoing conversation, "Hold your horses, folks! As thrilling as it is, the race is precisely scheduled for the day after my grand wedding extravaganza. Let's not get so engrossed in the roaring engines that we forget to dance at my wedding!"

The room erupted in laughter, echoing with amusement and agreement. It was a timely reminder that while the adrenaline of the race might be exhilarating, the joyous celebration of love and union was waiting just around the corner. The wedding, after all, was the main event, and Neetu made sure everyone had it on their mental calendar alongside the impending race.

CHAPTER 15

The Bachelorette!

Amidst the mounting excitement for Neetu's bachelorette, Vicky couldn't contain his enthusiasm. With a mischievous grin, he told his siblings, "Honestly, I'm more pumped up about this party than I am for the wedding or the car race combined!"

Neetu, Vicky and Jolly glanced at each other and began the plan.

Neetu enthusiastically said, "Dadaji, Momiji, we've got a surprise plan for Tracy and Sarah!"

Joginder Singh Ji, who was busy reading the newspaper on the chair, turned around and said, "Surprise? What's going on, beta?"

Vicky chimed in. "We're taking them to Dehradun as part of their India tour, you know?"

Amarjeet Kaur, raising an eyebrow, said, "Oh, sightseeing in Dehradun."

Neetu added, "And guess what? Tomorrow, we're heading to Rishikesh for river rafting! It's going to be epic!"

Joginder Singh smiled and said, "River rafting, huh? Well, as long as everyone stays safe."

Vicky displayed confidence. "Absolutely, Dadaji! It's going to be a blast."

Amarjeet Kaur, smirkingly, said, "And why didn't you mention this earlier?"

Jolly quickly added. "It was a last-minute plan, Dadiji. You know how these things are."

Joginder Singh nodded. "Alright, but take care of each other. And make sure Tracy and Sarah enjoy the trip."

As the group, fueled by excitement, prepared to leave, Amarjeet Kaur couldn't resist adding a parting remark.

Amarjeet Kaur said teasingly, "You kids and your impromptu plans! Have Fun, but be responsible. And bring Tracy and Sarah back safely!"

With laughter and promises of safety, the younger generation, led by Majid, set out on the journey to Dehradun, leaving the Singh household with a mix of anticipation and curiosity.

As the Singh youngsters sashayed out of the house, exuding an air of mischief and excitement, Vicky couldn't resist flashing a mischievous grin at Neetu. "Neetu! We're not forgetting your grand extravaganza. Majid Bhai, step on it! We've got a night of festivities waiting!"

Majid, behind the wheel, responded with a knowing smirk, revving the engine as if it were the prelude to an epic adventure.

Neetu, caught in the crossfire of anticipation and amusement, couldn't help but laugh. "Alright, Vicky, Majid Bhai, let's add some turbo to this celebration! Misadventures first, Wedding & Car Race later!"

Sarah, who was in the third-row seat with Tracy, said, "Folks, let's get back safe for the wedding!"

The SUV door slammed shut, sealing the pact of an unforgettable night. Little did they know, their journey was not just down winding roads but a rollercoaster of laughter, surprises, and a touch of unexpected events.

The engine roared to life, carrying the Singh youngsters to Dehradun, where the road to revelry awaited. Neetu's grand pre-wedding party stood as the beacon of joy at the end of the tunnel.

The air buzzed with excitement as the sun dipped behind the majestic mountains, casting a warm golden hue across the sprawling farmhouse. Guests, dressed in a kaleidoscope of colours, began to pour into the venue, greeted by the rhythmic beats of anticipation.

Sarah, with an air of confidence, was busy setting up her DJ console under a vibrant canopy. The tables adorned with flickering candles and fairy lights added a touch of enchantment to the evening. The sky, painted in hues of pink and orange, served as the perfect backdrop for what promised to be a night of revelry.

Majid, the master of ambience, had transformed the farmhouse into a pulsating haven of lights. Trance and disco lighting illuminated the surroundings, creating a mesmerising dance of colours that danced on the faces of the eager crowd. The scent of fragrant flowers and the sweet aroma of local delicacies wafted through the air, creating an intoxicating blend.

The heart of the celebration was the massive dance floor, a masterpiece by Majid himself. Flashing lights synchronised with the beats of the music, turning the dance floor into a canvas of movement and energy.

Laughter echoed as people mingled, clinking glasses in a toast to the night ahead.

The DJ console came to life as Sarah unleashed a torrent of music, the thumping bass echoing through the valley. Now filled with a kaleidoscope of twirling bodies, the dance floor became a stage for uninhibited joy.

Vicky, eyeing the spread of food, nudged Jolly with a playful grin. "Jolly, my man, did you personally supervise this feast, or did Majid Bhai recruit a team of culinary wizards?"

Jolly, holding a plate piled high with delicacies, chuckled. "Oh, you bet I did a taste test on everything. Majid Bhai might be the ambience maestro, but I'm the undisputed critic regarding food."

Jolly, pouring himself a drink, raised an eyebrow." And what about the drinks? Did you ensure the spirits are in high spirits?"

Vicky, taking a sip, said," Absolutely. We've got a concoction for every taste bud. Sarah even curated a playlist to complement the flavours. We're not just throwing a party but hosting a gastronomic and auditory extravaganza.

Vicky, clinking his glass against Jolly's, grinned, and both raised their glasses. "To Majid's lights, Sarah's beats, and your culinary expertise. Tonight, we feast and dance like there's no tomorrow."

The combination of the setting sun, the rhythmic beats, and the dazzling lights created an atmosphere that transported everyone to a realm of euphoria.

As the night unfolded, the farmstead came alive with laughter, music, and the shared joy of celebration. Majid's creation, a dance floor ablaze with lights, became the pulsating heart of the party, where memories were made under the canvas of the twilight sky.

The beats pulsated as Neetu lost in the party's rhythm. She was missing her fiance Yogesh and wished he could also join them.

Just then, she suddenly felt a tap on her shoulder. Turning around, her eyes widened in disbelief as she saw Yogesh standing there, a mischievous grin playing on his lips.

Yogesh smiled and said, "Missed me?"

Neetu, caught between surprise and sheer joy, could only manage a breathless nod. Vicky and Jolly, the masterminds behind this grand surprise, exchanged triumphant glances, revelling in the success of their plan.

Neetu stammered. "How... when... what?"

Vicky said with a grin, "Surprise, surprise! We thought the party needed a dash of extra magic."

Jolly chuckled. "And who better to bring the magic than the magician himself?"

Neetu, unable to contain her excitement, enveloped Yogesh in a tight hug.

Neetu had a hearty laugh. "You guys are unbelievable! How did you manage this?"

Yogesh glanced at her brothers. "Vicky and Jolly here are the masterminds. I just followed the script."

The party took on a new energy level as the crowd discovered Yogesh's unexpected presence. Ever the maestro, Sarah seized the moment and changed the rhythm to a soulful, romantic number. Neetu and Yogesh found themselves at the centre of attention, swaying to the music as if the world had melted away.

Sarah announced. "Ladies and gentlemen, let's give it up for the surprise guest and the soon-to-be-married couple!"

The dance floor transformed into a stage for love, the couple moving in perfect harmony. Neetu's eyes sparkled with happiness as Yogesh twirled her around, the flickering lights casting a magical glow on their faces.

The dance floor erupted in cheers and applause as Sarah played a unique romantic number. Neetu and Yogesh, lost in each other's eyes, danced as if the world had stopped just for them. Now infused with an extra dose of love, the party celebrated the night and the beautiful journey that led to this moment.

Amidst the joyous celebration on the dance floor, the entrance door swung open, and a figure stepped into the vibrant chaos. Ravi Chandra, Yogesh's good friend from Dehradun, sauntered in with an easy grin, catching the attention of Jolly, Vicky and Majid. Their carefree expressions tightened with a hint of surprise.

Yogesh, spotting Ravi, couldn't contain his excitement. "Look who decided to join the party! Everyone, meet Ravi, my partner in crime from Dehradun."

As Yogesh introduced Ravi to the gathering, Jolly exchanged a quick, concerned glance with Vicky. The duo knew Ravi as a fierce competitor in the mountain race they were preparing for. The tension in the air became palpable, concealed beneath the veneer of smiles and greetings.

Trying to keep it light, Vicky extended a hand to Ravi with a forced smile. "Welcome, Ravi! Heard a lot about you."

Ravi said with a grin on his face, "Likewise! Pleasure meeting the Singhs."

Jolly, with a concealed smirk, chimed in. He tried to sound casual. "Well, Dehradun must be an exciting place with friends like you."

As the night progressed, the music grew louder, and the once-refined dance floor turned into a swirling sea of laughter and inebriation.

Glasses clinked, and the atmosphere was charged with the spirit of celebration. Amid the revelry, Ravi Chandar, fueled by the elixir of merriment, stumbled upon Sarah and Tracy, who were swaying to the beats.

Ravi spoke with a slur. "Well, well, if it isn't the life of the party!"

Neetu, who was standing nearby, decided to play the role of the introducer.

"Ravi, meet Sarah and Tracy. They're our distant relatives from the US."

Ravi, squinting with an alcohol-induced haze, looked at the two girls with a lackadaisical grin and chuckled. "Tapinder Singh, eh? That guy left the family behind, went to the US, and never returned. Classic!"

Sarah and Tracy exchanged uncomfortable glances, their smiles fading as Ravi's words hung like a bitter aftertaste. Neetu, sensing the sudden shift in mood, tried to lighten it.

Neetu nervously said, "Oh, Ravi, it's all good. It's fun. Let's not get too serious."

But Ravi, under the influence of the potent mix of alcohol and candour, continued his tirade.

Ravi said in a mocking tone, "Fun, huh? Yeah, your uncle Tapinder knows how to have a good time, leaving everyone behind to party in the States."

With a forced smile, Sarah spoke up, her voice tinged with sadness. "He had his reasons, Ravi. It's not as simple as it seems."

The tension in the air escalated with each word, and as Ravi's sarcastic remarks cut through the celebration, Jolly, who had been standing a few feet away, couldn't hold back any longer.

His eyes ablaze with fury, Jolly stormed into the conversation, grabbing Ravi's collar with a vice-like grip. "Watch your mouth, Ravi! This is a party, not your personal boxing ring."

Ravi, unyielding, shot back with a string of insults, each word a spark that fueled the growing fire. "Oh, what's the matter, Jolly? Can't handle a little truth? Sore loser, aren't you?

Jolly snapped like a taut wire and swung a blow at Ravi's face in a rage. The impact echoed through the party, drawing gasps from the onlookers. The verbal confrontation had now erupted into a full-blown physical altercation.

Ravi, nursing his stinging cheek, retaliated with a vengeance.

As the two grappled, fists flying, Ravi, fueled by the liquid courage coursing through his veins, declared with a sinister smirk. "You think you can beat me in the race this year? I've owned those mountain roads for the past three years, Jolly. You're no competition."

Jolly, clenched in frustration, shot back with an intensity that matched the bitterness in the air. He unleashed a mighty blow that sent Ravi staggering.

In a desperate attempt to regain his balance, Ravi, in a moment of blind rage, thrust out his leg, catching Jolly off guard.

With a sickening crash, Jolly toppled backwards, landing on a nest of lights and wires at the side of the party area. The night erupted into chaos as the lights flickered ominously, and Jolly lay unconscious, a victim of the violent clash.

Panic gripped the scene as partygoers rushed to his aid, realising the festive atmosphere had turned dark.

In the mayhem, Majid frantically rushed out to bring the car.

Vicky, Neetu, Tracy and Sarah watched with shock and fear as Jolly's lifeless form sprawled amidst the tangled wires.

The chaotic night had transformed into a sombre scene as Majid and the Singh youngsters rushed Jolly to the nearby hospital. The air inside the car was thick with worry, the distant sounds of the party now replaced by the hum of the engine and the weight of an unforeseen tragedy.

Majid, driving with urgency, glanced at the unconscious Jolly in the rearview mirror. Neetu, Sarah, Vicky, and Tracy were silent, their minds racing with concern and guilt over the events.

As they reached the hospital, Majid and the youngsters navigated through the sterile halls to the emergency room, where medical staff took charge of Jolly's care. Majid, his face a mask of concern, paced outside the room, silently praying for Jolly's well-being.

The real challenge, however, awaited them at home. The Singh youngsters knew they had to face the daunting task of informing their parents and grandparents about the incident. The joyous celebration had morphed into a situation that demanded courage and delicate handling of emotions.

Majid, Neetu, Sarah, Vicky, and Tracy gathered in a hushed conversation, contemplating how to break the news.

Tracy, her voice quivering, spoke up. "We can't keep this from them. We need to tell our folks back home."

Sarah nodded in agreement, her eyes reflecting the weight of the situation. "We owe them the truth, no matter how difficult."

With a heavy heart, Neetu called Joginder Singh Ji.

Back at the Singh residence, the atmosphere was still festive. They were unaware of the tragedy that had befallen one of their own. The news hit them like a sudden storm, shattering the atmosphere of merriment.

Neetu, her voice steady but laced with concern. "Dadaji, there's something we need to talk about."

Sensing the gravity in Neetu's tone, Joginder Singh Ji got up from his seat. "What is it, beta?"

Neetu conveyed the news with a heavy heart. "There was an accident. Jolly... Jolly got hurt. We've rushed him to the hospital in Dehradun."

A palpable silence descended upon him as Joginder Singh Ji processed the information.

The Singh Elders rallied together in haste. The car ride to the hospital was a journey filled with an ominous silence, the weight of uncertainty hanging in the air. They arrived at the hospital in Dehradun with their faces etched with concern.

The waiting area of the hospital, usually a place of anticipation, now bore witness to the collective anxiety of a family bonded by blood and love.

The family huddled together, seeking strength from one another, as they waited for news about Jolly. Time seemed to stretch, each moment an eternity, until a doctor finally emerged to provide an update.

A sigh of relief swept through the Singh family as the Doctor emerged with the long-awaited update. "I have good news. Jolly is stable; he'll regain consciousness shortly. However, his right leg sustained burns from the electrical shock. We'll need to perform surgery to ensure a proper recovery."

Joginder Singh Ji's eyes, filled with worry just moments ago, now brimmed with gratitude. "Thank you, Doctor. When can we see him?"

Doctor responded. "In a short while. The surgery is scheduled, and he'll be in the recovery room soon."

Neetu, Sarah, Vicky, and Tracy exchanged glances, their faces reflecting the mix of anxiety and relief. The weight that had hung in the air lifted, replaced by a sense of hope.

Rekha and Tannu, their eyes reflecting a blend of concern and hope, leaned in towards the Doctor, their voices soft yet desperate for reassurance. "Jolly will be fine, naa Doctor? Tell us he'll be back to his mischievous self soon."

The Doctor confirmed, "The surgery is routine, and he should return to his feet with proper care in a few weeks.

Amarjeet Kaur said, "Thank you, Doctor. We appreciate your efforts."

As the Doctor retreated, the Singh family, though still fraught with concern for Jolly, felt a renewed sense of optimism. The waiting room, once a space filled with tension, now echoed with murmurs of gratitude and whispered prayers.

Joginder Singh Ji addressed the family. "Let's stay strong for Jolly. He'll need our support in the days to come."

The family nodded in unison, their bond fortified by the shared relief that their beloved Jolly was on the path to recovery. The waiting room became a sanctuary of hope. As they prepared to see Jolly, the Singh family braced themselves for the healing journey ahead.

The Singh youngsters gathered, faces etched with guilt and apprehension. The elders, including Joginder Singh Ji, sat patiently

curious, sensing that something was amiss.

Neetu, taking a deep breath, broke the uneasy silence nervously. "We need to talk about the pre-wedding party."

Joginder Singh Ji, with raised eyebrows, said, "What happened, beta?"

Tracy and Sarah exchanged glances, their expressions revealing a shared burden.

Sarah said apologetically. "We have something to confess. It was a pre-wedding party, not sightseeing as we had told you."

Tracy joined in. "We orchestrated a secret dance party".

Joginder Singh Ji's stern expression softened, replaced by a curious gaze. "Why the deception?"

Vicky quickly added, "We just wanted to add an extra excitement to the celebrations, a little adventure."

Neetu said with a regretful tone. "We should've been honest from the start, but the thrill got the better of us."

Vicky took responsibility and said, "It was our idea. Sarah and Tracy just helped us to keep the plan under wraps."

Sarah apologised. "We're sorry for lying, Dadaji and everyone. It wasn't our intention to cause any distress."

After contemplating, Joginder Singh Ji broke into a warm smile. "Well, you certainly added some spice to the festivities. Lying is not ideal, but your heart is in the right place. Let's just ensure we keep honesty at the forefront from now on."

The atmosphere shifted from tension to relief as forgiveness and understanding permeated the room. The elders, recognising the genuine intentions behind the youngsters' actions, embraced them with a spirit of forgiveness.

Neetu took a deep breath and continued recounting the events of the night. "The fight between Ravi and Jolly... it escalated quickly. It was intense, and in the midst of it, Jolly lost his balance and fell onto the wires."

Vicky, his face a mix of concern and anger, spoke up. "Dadaji, we should file a police case against Ravi for what he did to Jolly. It was no accident; it was an assault."

Joginder Singh Ji, though visibly upset, maintained a calm demeanour.

"Vicky, I understand your concern, but we must consider the circumstances. It happened in the heat of the moment, and filing a police case may complicate matters further."

Vicky persisted. "But, Dadaji, Jolly got seriously hurt. We can't just let this slide."

Joginder Singh Ji responded, "Retaliation won't heal Jolly faster, beta. We should address this issue in another way. I know how exactly we'll teach Ravi Chandar a lesson."

Neetu added. "Dadaji is right. Let's focus on Jolly's recovery first. We can sort out the rest later. And my wedding functions are going to start tomorrow. Please don't spoil them!"

Unable to shake off his frustration, Vicky observed: "Dadaji, something is bothering me. Yogesh brought Ravi Chandar to the party. After what happened to Jolly, he's least bothered to enquire about him."

Just then, Yogesh entered the waiting area, sensing the palpable tension in the air. His eyes quickly scanned the faces of the Singh family, and he immediately recognised the gravity of the situation and asked. "How's Jolly?"

Vicky, still feeling frustrated, spoke up. "You should be asking that question for your friend Ravi Chandar, not here."

His expression shifting to a mix of guilt and concern, Yogesh approached Joginder Singh Ji. "Dadaji, I'm sorry. Since Ravi is my friend. I take full responsibility for what happened."

Joginder Singh Ji, though stern, nodded in acknowledgement of Yogesh's apology.

Neetu, touched by Yogesh's sincerity, stepped forward and hugged him.

As Yogesh expressed remorse, the room shifted from tension to a tentative sense of resolution.

The complexities of friendship and family loyalty hung in the air. Still, Yogesh's willingness to take responsibility and seek forgiveness from the Singh family offered a glimmer of hope for reconciliation and healing.

After contemplating, Joginder Singh Ji addressed Yogesh with a firm yet understanding tone. "Yogesh, go home. The wedding functions are set to begin, and we shouldn't let this incident dilute the joyous celebrations. Jolly is in capable hands, and we'll ensure he gets the care he needs."

Yogesh, grateful for the consideration, nodded. "Thank you, Dadaji. I'll ensure everything is taken care of, and I'll be there in Behalpur to seek your blessings and take Neetu home."

CHAPTER 16

Let the Wedding Festivities Begin!

The wedding festivities had begun, and Behalpur echoed with the sounds of celebration. The air was filled with the fragrance of flowers, and the vibrant colours of joy adorned every corner. Yet, amidst the laughter and music, Neetu was torn between the elation of her impending nuptials and the sombre reality of her brother's condition.

The radiant glow of vibrant lights adorned the Singh residence, announcing the commencement of Neetu and Yogesh's wedding week.

The air crackled with excitement, and the first notes of joy were struck with the Sangeet function—a celebration deeply embedded in the cultural fabric of North India.

The word "sangeet," resonating with the melodic essence of the song, embodied the heart and soul of this pre-wedding ceremony.

Traditionally, it was a female-only affair, meticulously organised by the bride and groom's families to honour and celebrate the bride a few days before the grand wedding ceremony.

The Singh residence transformed into a kaleidoscope of colours, laughter, and music as the Sangeet unfolded. The rhythmic beats of dhols resonated through the air, inviting everyone to join in the festivities.

With their timeless melodies, the historical custom of singing folk songs echoed the joyous anticipation of the impending union.

The heart of the celebration lay in the spirited dancing, as family members and friends, their hearts intertwined with the cadence of tradition, formed a lively dance floor.

The energy was infectious, and the night became a canvas upon which the joy of the imminent union was painted with every twirl and step.

In recent times, the Sangeet has evolved. Couples now take centre stage, hosting the night together and weaving their tales of love through choreographed Bollywood performances.

The celebration is no longer confined to gender lines; it's an inclusive jubilation where families and friends unite to honour the couple and their journey ahead.

The stage was set aglow with a cascade of colourful lights as family members prepared for their performances at Neetu and Yogesh's Sangeet.

Laughter echoed in the air, and the excitement was palpable as each member of the Singh family eagerly took their place in the spotlight.

Tracy and Sarah, the dynamic duo, stepped onto the stage to the beats of a popular Punjabi song that had everyone in the audience tapping their feet. The lyrics resonated through the venue, and the song's infectious energy set the tone for a lively performance.

As the music took over, Tracy and Sarah, dressed in vibrant Punjabi suits, began to dance with exuberance. Their synchronised moves mirrored the spirit of the lyrics, and their joyous expressions radiated happiness. The crowd couldn't help but be drawn into the magnetic energy of their performance.

The lyrics echoed through the venue as Tracy and Sarah swirled and twirled: "Mainu Lengha Laide Mehnga

Jeya Marjaneya, Aine Paise Das Tu Kithe Laike Jaane Aa..."

The crowd applauded as Tracy and Sarah blended traditional Punjabi dance moves with contemporary flair. The stage, alive with the song's rhythm, became a vibrant spectacle of celebration, showcasing the unity and joy within the Singh family.

The stage shimmered in a soft glow as Neetu and Yogesh, the bride and groom, took centre stage for a mesmerising performance.

The atmosphere buzzed with anticipation, and the audience held their breath as the opening notes of the romantic Bollywood song "Teri Ore" began to play.

Neetu, draped in an ethereal lehenga, and Yogesh, handsomely attired in traditional attire, moved in perfect harmony. Their chemistry was palpable, and the song's lyrics echoed the emotions that blossomed between them.

"Teri Ore, Teri Ore, Teri Ore, hai Rabba..." As the music enveloped them, Neetu and Yogesh glided across the stage with grace, mirroring the ebb and flow of the lyrics. The dance became a poetic expression of love, with every step and gesture conveying the depth of their connection.

The audience was captivated by the tenderness in their movements and how they looked at each other, lost in the moment's magic. The romantic melody resonated through the venue, creating an enchanting ambience that seemed to suspend time.

The performance seamlessly transitioned into a medley of romantic Bollywood songs, each a chapter in their love story. The lyrics became a silent dialogue, expressing the unspoken feelings that had brought Neetu and Yogesh to this moment.

As they twirled and swayed, the audience became enraptured by the love story unfolding before them. The dance was not just a performance but a celebration of the journey that had led Neetu and Yogesh to the threshold of matrimony.

The applause erupted as the last notes faded, a testament to their performance's beauty. Neetu and Yogesh, hand in hand, basked in the glow of their shared love, marking the Sangeet with a dance that etched their romance into the hearts of everyone present.

Neetu and Yogesh, surrounded by the laughter and love of their dear ones, embraced the Sangeet as a prelude to their grand wedding. On this night, tradition, melody, and dance converged to mark the onset of a new, joyous journey together.

The tempo of the evening soared as the spotlight shifted to the patriarch of the Singh family, Joginder Singh Ji. The audience cheered as he gracefully took the stage, exuding a timeless charm. Amarjeet Kaur, his partner in this dance, joined him with a radiant smile.

The opening notes of "Ae Meri Zohrajabeen" filled the air. With a twinkle in his eye, Joginder Singh Ji led Amarjeet Kaur into a dance that set the stage ablaze. The classic melody echoed through the venue, creating an atmosphere of nostalgia and celebration.

As they moved together, Joginder Singh Ji showcased a flair for dance that surprised and delighted the audience. The chemistry between him and Amarjeet Kaur was a testament to the enduring romance that had weathered the sands of time.

As the song's final notes rang out, thunderous applause followed. Joginder Singh Ji and Amarjeet Kaur, with smiles mirrored a lifetime of shared moments, basked in the warmth of the audience's appreciation.

Their dance wasn't just a performance but a celebration of enduring love and the spirit of togetherness. The stage, now lit with the afterglow of their enchanting performance, became a canvas upon which the essence of family, love, and celebration converged.

As the night reached its crescendo, the stage was set for the final dance performance. This spectacle would weave together the threads of celebration and camaraderie. However, a sudden turn of events confined Jolly to the hospital, leaving his dancing shoes unfilled.

In a heartwarming gesture, Majid stepped into the spotlight, ready to take on the role of Jolly for this exceptional performance alongside Vicky. The audience, aware of the impromptu change, embraced the moment with open hearts.

Vicky and Majid, a dynamic duo in their own right, kicked off the performance with Bollywood dance numbers. However, the lack of coordination in their steps was evident, and it was clear that Majid was graciously filling Jolly's shoes at the last moment. Yet, their infectious energy and the spirit of improvisation created a unique charm that resonated with everyone present.

The stage, aglow with a kaleidoscope of lights, witnessed Vicky and Majid dancing to the rhythm of iconic Bollywood tunes. Laughter echoed through the venue as the two friends poured their enthusiasm into every step despite the lack of synchronised moves.

Photos and videos of the performance were swiftly shared with Jolly, who enjoyed the event virtually despite being confined to a hospital bed. The camaraderie and joy captured in those moments were a testament to the resilience of friendships and the ability to find laughter even in unexpected circumstances.

As the performance concluded, the applause was for the dance and the spirit of togetherness woven through the entire Sangeet night. The shared moments, whether on the stage or behind a screen, became treasured memories that would be etched in the hearts of the Singh family, a testament to the power of love, celebration, and the enduring bonds of family and friendship.

The following day dawned with a golden hue as the Singh residence buzzed with excitement for Neetu and Yogesh's engagement. The air was filled with anticipation, and the decor exuded an aura of grandeur, befitting the occasion's significance.

In the evening, as Neetu and Yogesh stood before the gathering, surrounded by the warmth of family and friends, the exchange of rings marked the formal sealing of their commitment. The sparkle of the engagement rings mirrored the radiant smiles on the couple's faces, and the air was charged with the promise of a shared future.

The engagement ceremony unfolded with a cascade of gifts, a tangible expression of love and blessings. Neetu and Yogesh were showered with affection tokens, symbolising their well-wishers' collective joy and support.

The highlight of the gift-giving extravaganza was the show of gold ornaments for Neetu. Elaborate necklaces, bangles, and earrings adorned her, each piece a testament to the opulence and heartfelt blessings bestowed upon the bride. The room shimmered with the reflection of gold, creating an ethereal ambience that added to the grandeur of the celebration.

Amidst the joyous engagement ceremony, Vicky, Majid, and Sarah found a moment to huddle together, their expressions mixing curiosity and speculation.

Vicky spoke to Majid and Sarah. "Have you noticed something strange?

Ravi Chandar is nowhere to be seen. No dance, no greetings—nothing."

Sarah, chiming in with a mischievous smile, added her perspective.

"Maybe he got cold feet after what happened at Dehradun."

Majid said with a smirk. "Or maybe, just maybe, he's busy tuning up his car for the upcoming race."

Sarah laughed. "Well, if that's the case, he's missing out on one heck of a celebration."

The trio shared a conspiratorial glance, revelling in the playful speculation about Ravi Chandar's absence. The engagement ceremony continued in full swing, but the mystery of Ravi's whereabouts added an intriguing element to the festivities.

Little did they know that the unfolding events would weave an exciting tale.

CHAPTER 17

The Wedding

The wedding evening arrived in a burst of colours and jubilation; the air was alive with the beats of dhol and the joyful laughter of the attendees. The sun dipped low on the horizon, casting a warm glow over the festivities as Neetu, the bride, embarked on the final stages of her bridal preparations.

Neetu was transformed into a vision of grace and beauty in a room adorned with marigold garlands and fragrant jasmine. The rustle of her turquoise lehenga and the tinkling of her jewellery echoed the excitement that filled the air.

"Nazar na lage tujhe!". Grandmother Amarjeet Kaur exclaimed. "Sarah and Tracy, you look stunning in the lehengas. Wish Tapinder was here to see you in this avatar."

Sarah and Tracy felt nostalgic, remembering the days when they would celebrate Indian festivals in New York wearing traditional Indian clothes.

"Mom," Sarah exclaimed with pride and delight, "look at this! It's not just a design; it's a piece of art, a celebration etched on my hands." The rich, brown hues of the Mehendi stood out in stark contrast against her fair skin, creating a mesmerising pattern.

Tracy, touched by the intricate beauty, traced the designs with a gentle finger, her eyes reflecting a shared joy.

Sarah turned to Neetu, a soft smile on her lips. She whispered, "You look gorgeous in your favourite Turquoise Lehenga as if an Apsara has descended on the earth today."

Neetu responded with a bubbly laugh, "Oh, thank you, Sarah! I can already picture you turning heads at my wedding, and who knows, you might end up with a stack of marriage proposals! Just hoping Yogesh doesn't spot you; otherwise, he might have second thoughts about marrying me!"

Neetu and Sarah burst into infectious laughter, enjoying the playful banter and sharing a moment of light-hearted joy.

Keenly observant, Tracy couldn't help but notice the glistening tears that welled up in Rekha's eyes. She gently approached her, a quiet understanding passing between them and said softly. "Does today's Neetu bring back memories of your wedding, Rekha?"

Rekha, her gaze momentarily lost in the past, spoke with a heavy heart, the weight of emotions evident in her voice. "Yes Tracy, today echoes with the echoes of my wedding day. But, more than that, it stirs a profound sadness within me—knowing that Neetu will soon leave the warmth of our home."

Sensing the depth of Rekha's emotions, Sarah gently intervened, offering a perspective rooted in the optimism of the present age. "Rekha Aunty, we live in a world where distances seem to shrink daily. Besides, Dehradun is just an hour away from here."

Rekha acknowledged the reality with a bittersweet smile but couldn't shake off the ache in her heart. "I understand, Sarah, but things will never be the same. Life has a way of claiming its own space, and as she steps into her new journey, Neetu will inevitably get entwined in her own life."

At that moment, the room was filled with spoken words and the silent echoes of shared emotions. Neetu's impending departure served as a poignant reminder that, even in a hyper-connected world, the ties that bind are enduring and fragile.

As Neetu awaited the grand entrance of her prince, Yogesh, the atmosphere outside pulsed with energy.

The groom, dressed regally in traditional attire, mounted a majestic horse, capturing the essence of a modern-day prince. His family and friends surrounded him, adding to the spectacle of the grand baraat.

The procession moved forward with the rhythmic beats of the dhol, and the lively tunes of Punjabi folk songs filled the air. The groom's dancing and celebrating entourage created a vibrant parade that meandered through the streets. The joyous atmosphere was contagious, with onlookers joining the revelry, and the celebration became a moving spectacle of exuberance.

Behind the adorned horse that carried the groom, family and friends danced in joy, creating a lively backdrop to the procession. The cars that followed the horse served as a mobile bar counter. The car's windows rolled down, and laughter mingled with the music, with occasional toasts and cheers for the soon-to-be-wed couple.

The groom, astride the horse, took on the role of the charismatic leader, waving to the onlookers with a smile that mirrored the joyous spirit of the occasion. The journey to the wedding venue became a fusion of tradition and modernity. This procession celebrated love and union in the most jubilant manner.

As the entourage reached the wedding venue, the anticipation reached its peak. Neetu, adorned in all her bridal glory, awaited the arrival of her charming prince. The grand baraat, a blend of traditional rituals and contemporary celebration, symbolised the union of two families and the promise of a joyous journey ahead.

The Singh family awaited the groom's arrival, ready to extend a warm and formal reception.

As Yogesh's party reached the entrance, they were formally greeted by the bride's side with vibrant garlands, lit candles, and vermillion bindis, symbolising the auspicious beginning of the wedding festivities.

Amidst the cheerful atmosphere, a light-hearted tradition unfolded—the groom, accompanied by his friends and cousins, had to part with some money to enter the wedding venue. Neetu's siblings and cousins, mischievous smiles playing on their faces, playfully negotiated the entry fee, adding a touch of humour and camaraderie to the proceedings.

Neetu's Cousin-Sister-1 spoke with a mischievous glint in her eyes, "Well, well, it seems we've got a VIP gracing us with his presence. Entrance fee, anyone?"

With a confident smirk, Yogesh retorted, "What's the price of admission, then?"

Neetu's Cousin-Sister-2 teasingly responded, "Oh, just a modest contribution to the 'Let-Yogesh-In-Fund.'"

Yogesh played along, humour lacing his words, "Modest, huh? Let's hope my wallet can bear the burden."

Just then, the atmosphere shifted as Ravi Chandar made his entrance.

Turning towards Yogesh, Sarah said wryly, "Speak of the devil, and Ravi's here."

Ignoring Sarah's comment, Ravi entered with an air of nonchalance, "Well, well, well! What's the toll for today?"

Neetu's Cousin-Sister-2 interrupted, "Oh, Ravi, you're fashionably late, as always. We were just discussing the exclusive entrance fee for our VIP groom. Unfortunately, you seem to have missed the bus."

Rolling his eyes, Vicky injected a touch of sarcasm, "Oh, Ravi, discounts are exclusively for friends and family. You might need a coupon for that."

Ravi, undeterred, tried to direct his charm towards Sarah: "Hey, Sarah, you're looking stunning as always. Are you considering marrying a handsome guy like me?"

Skillfully avoiding the attempt at flattery, Sarah continued with a playful silence.

Things took a turn when Ravi, pushing boundaries, invaded Sarah's personal space. Majid, unable to contain his irritation, intervened with a touch of humour, "Easy there, Ravi. Can you please back off? You're starting to smell like engine oil."

Laughter rippled through the crowd.

Ravi, now angered, questioned Majid, "What's your problem?"

Standing his ground, Majid asserted, "Just respecting personal space, my friend."

Adopting a warning tone, Ravi declared, "You guys are playing with fire. Remember what happened to Jolly? Don't push it too far."

A momentary hush fell over the group, the weight of Ravi's words lingering before laughter erupted again. This was a collective response to the delicate dance between humour and caution.

Just then, Yogesh pushed inside and handed over bundles of cash to Neetu's sisters, and the groom's family made their way inside.

The Joota Chupai custom further added to the playful antics. As Yogesh prepared for the wedding ceremony, Neetu's sisters and female relatives seized the opportunity to engage in a spirited game of hiding the groom's shoes. The laughter echoed as Yogesh's shoes were playfully concealed, and the demand for a ransom rang through the air. In good spirits, Yogesh indulged in the tradition, offering a delightful dance and contributing to the shoe fund, enhancing the joyful ambience of the celebration.

As the Baraat festivities reached a crescendo, Neetu made her grand entrance, heralded by her parents, family, and close friends. The Kanya Aagaman, or the bride's arrival, was a moment of profound beauty. Neetu, adorned in resplendent bridal attire, was traditionally carried in a Dolhi by her brothers and male cousins. Majid also joined the tradition.

The Doli symbolised grace and regality, creating a stunning visual spectacle from a simple canopy to an ornate carriage. Over her head, they held a large mesh of fresh flowers, adding a fragrant touch to the ceremonial procession.

The mingling of traditions and joy, punctuated by playful rituals, set the stage for a wedding celebration that embraced the occasion's solemnity and exuberance.

Under the expansive canopy of a vibrant mandap, Neetu and Yogesh embarked on the sacred journey of marriage. The air was infused with the fragrance of marigolds and the rhythmic chants of the priest, setting the stage for a union steeped in tradition and love.

With the resonance of ancient prayers, the priest guided them through the sacred rituals. The exchange of garlands, a symbol of mutual respect and acceptance, marked the initial steps of their journey together. Each petal and thread woven into the garlands whispered promises of unity and companionship.

The couple then started circling the agni (holy fire) as the priest chanted the Mantras. Yogesh led Neetu on the first few feras (Circles). At the same time, Neetu took over for the final step, symbolising balance in their marriage.

With a gentle solemnity, Yogesh tied the auspicious mangal sutra around Neetu's neck, symbolising their sacred bond forging. The golden threads intertwined, signifying the eternal connection between husband and wife and the beginning of a shared destiny.

As the ceremony progressed, Yogesh, with the utmost reverence, applied sindoor on Neetu's forehead. The vermillion, vibrant against her glowing skin, symbolised the deep-rooted commitment and marital bliss they were invoking.

The culmination of the ceremony saw Neetu and Yogesh taking blessings from each other's families. This poignant moment bridged the two worlds they were uniting. The elders blessed the couple and wished them a life of love, prosperity, and understanding.

The sacred ceremony unfolded under the watchful gaze of camera drones, capturing every nuance and emotion as Neetu and Yogesh embarked on their marital journey. The whirring hum of the drones above became silent witnesses to the timeless rituals.

In an era where technology seamlessly blends with tradition, the ceremony was broadcast on the local cable network of Behalpur. The vibrant colours, the resonant chants, and the tender moments were beamed into the community's homes, uniting the town in the joyous celebration.

Simultaneously, the sacred union was live-streamed on YouTube and Instagram, transcending geographical boundaries and inviting well-wishers from across the globe to participate in the festivities.

The chat section overflowed with congratulatory messages and virtual blessings as friends and family, near and far, joined in the jubilation.

Amidst the viewership, one spectator held a special place—Jolly, still recuperating in the hospital. The live transmission brought the essence of the wedding directly to his bedside. The glowing screen transported him to the mandap, allowing him to witness the love, laughter, and sacred vows that echoed through the pixels.

Neetu found moments of serenity to capture the magic of her wedding day. With her phone in hand, she artfully took selfies, each click reflecting the radiant glow of a bride immersed in the warmth of love. Her eyes sparkled with happiness, and the intricate details of her bridal attire became a canvas for the lens.

Drawing Yogesh into the frame, they posed together, their smiles telling the story of a shared journey beginning anew. The chemistry between them, captured in each snapshot, spoke volumes of the love that had blossomed into matrimony.

Eager to share these precious moments, Neetu swiftly uploaded the pictures onto her Instagram handle. The virtual world became a gallery of emotions as friends, family, and well-wishers flooded the comments section with congratulations and heart emojis.

Through the lens of social media, Neetu invited the world to celebrate her union with Yogesh. The digital album became a testament to their love story, a visual diary that transcended time, allowing the memories of this special day to be cherished and revisited with just a scroll and tap.

The fusion of tradition and technology allowed the magic of the wedding to reach far beyond the physical confines of Behalpur, uniting hearts and souls in the celebration of Neetu and Yogesh's union.

Once all the photo sessions with family members were done, it was time for Neetu and Yogesh to leave; under the soft glow of twinkling stars, Neetu stood adorned in bridal grace, a poignant moment in the fabric of time when tradition dictated her departure from the haven of her family.

The words "Taron ki chhaon mein" whispered through the air, carrying the weight of centuries-old traditions, the echo of countless brides bidding farewell. The night, once resplendent with celebration, now cradled a bittersweet farewell.

Neetu's eyes sparkled with the remnants of joy and the glistening of tears as she prepared to embrace a new home and life. Beside her stood Yogesh, his eyes reflecting both the love for his bride and a solemn understanding of the moment's gravity.

Once alive with laughter and music, the wedding venue became a silent witness to a sacred ritual—a daughter's departure. Like witnesses from generations past, the stars above bore witness to the timeless ceremony unfolding below.

Neetu's parents, flanked by the glow of oil lamps, stood with hearts heavy and eyes moist. Their little girl, now a bride, was about to embark on a journey leading her away from the comforting cocoon of their love and care. The air was charged with unspoken emotions, a symphony of joy and sorrow, love and letting go.

As Neetu took each step, the fragrance of marigolds and the soft rustle of her bridal attire marked the passage into a new chapter. The shadows of the night seemed to embrace her while the gentle breeze carried the whispered blessings of her family.

Each footfall echoed the heartbeat of a daughter leaving her childhood home, embracing an unknown yet promising future.

Understanding the moment's gravity, Yogesh walked beside Neetu, a pillar of strength, silently promising to be the foundation of her new world. Like celestial witnesses, the stars above adorned the sky with brilliance, casting a starry canopy over the departing bride.

The departure was not just from a physical space but a spiritual transition, a rite of passage. The tears that welled in the eyes of both Neetu and her parents were not just symbols of parting but also of the profound love and connection that would endure across distances.

As Neetu's silhouette merged with the night, a collective sigh seemed to escape from the hearts of those left behind.

In a thrilling crescendo to the emotional departure, a sports car adorned with flowers and gleaming in the night roared to a screeching halt outside the venue.

The unexpected arrival added an electrifying spark to the poignant scene. As the dust settled, the driver's seat revealed a familiar face—none other than Ravi Chandar.

With a sheepish grin directed at Vicky, Sarah, and Majid, Ravi emerged, ready to play a surprising role in Neetu and Yogesh's journey.

Gesturing with flair, he welcomed the newlyweds into the back seat, making the car a symbol of departure and adventure.

Ravi stepped out of the car and boldly declared to the Singh Family, "This car is carrying the Dulhania now, and in a few hours from now, it will transform into a thundering beast to conquer the mountain race with unmatched speed."

The Singhs were taken aback. The unexpected twist left everyone in astonishment and excitement, a fitting climax to a night woven with threads of tradition and surprises.

As the resonating echoes of Ravi Chandar's declaration lingered in the air, Joginder Singh Ji, the patriarch of the Singh family, stepped forward with a determined gleam in his eyes.

The atmosphere crackled with anticipation as Joginder Ji, with unwavering conviction, declared, "Majid would break Ravi's victory streak and triumph over him on his own home ground."

Ravi Chandar, upon hearing Joginder Singh Ji's bold challenge, smirked with confidence that bordered on arrogance. He retorted, "Well, Joginder Singh Ji, it seems the Singh family is eager to spice up the race. I've owned these mountain roads for years, and Majid stepping into the arena won't change the inevitable outcome."

Joginder Singh Ji clapped Majid on the back with a hearty laugh and said, "You're filling Jolly's shoes, my boy! It's time to show Ravi what the Singh family is made of!"

Still processing the unexpected turn of events, Majid stammered, "Wait, what? Me? Race? Tomorrow?"

Little did Majid know that he had unwittingly become the unexpected hero of the upcoming mountain race.

As the weight of Joginder Singh Ji's words sank in, a resolute determination replaced the initial shock on Majid's face. His gaze, once bewildered, now held a steely focus.

The mountain race had transformed from an unexpected obligation into a mission — a chance to avenge Jolly's injury and rectify the indignation Ravi Chandar had inflicted on Sarah.

CHAPTER 18

The Race Day

After the emotional wedding festivities and the unexpected revelation of Majid's participation in the mountain race, the Singh household was anything but tranquil.

The patriarch, Joginder Singh, noticing the collective lack of sleep, urged everyone to catch a few hours of rest. However, Majid and the younger cousins were far from ready to surrender to slumber. Gathered in a hushed corner, they huddled together, their eyes reflecting determination and trepidation.

On a video call, Jolly, still recuperating from his injury, joined the impromptu strategy session. The gravity of the impending race hung in the air as Majid unveiled a secret weapon — a supercharged modification he had discreetly installed in the car just days before. It was an untested addition, left dormant due to Jolly's injury.

"I didn't think we'd be racing, especially with Jolly in this condition," Majid confessed. "But this supercharge needs testing, and the race is the only way."

Despite the physical distance, Jolly injected a note of enthusiasm into the conversation. "Let's not hold back, Majid. We're in this to win, not just for me but for the Singh legacy."

As the dawn light gradually spilt over the horizon, the Singh youngsters delved into the intricacies of their race strategy. A unified resolve emerged amid discussions of turns, accelerations, and potential challenges.

The race wasn't just a competition but a quest for redemption, a chance to assert the Singh family's prowess against the arrogant and egoistic Ravi Chandar.

Amidst the pre-race strategising, Sarah, known for her upbeat spirit, noticed the faint traces of concern on Majid's face. With a warm smile, she stepped forward, her words a beacon of encouragement for him.

"Majid, you've got this," Sarah asserted, her eyes reflecting unwavering confidence. "We've seen you handle challenges before, and this race is no different. Remember, you're not just driving for yourself; you're driving for the

Singh legacy and for Jolly. This is our chance to show Ravi Chandar that the Singh family is a force to be reckoned with."

She placed a reassuring hand on Majid's shoulder, conveying solidarity. "You've got a supercharge under that hood, and it's not just about testing it. It's about unveiling it in a spectacular triumph. We believe in you, Majid. Let the mountains witness the roar of your determination, leaving Ravi Chandar trailing behind."

Majid, touched by the sincerity in Sarah's words, nodded with a newfound determination.

As the decisive moment approached, Amarjeet Kaur orchestrated a swift symphony in the kitchen, crafting a hearty breakfast and invigorating tea for the challenge ahead.

Fueled by the nourishing meal, everyone readied themselves for the ascent into the mountains.

Majid took the driver's seat in the Singh Sports car, flanked by the unwavering support of Vicky, Sarah, and Tracy.

The elders, including Joginder Singh, stayed home, expressing hope and trust.

As Majid revved the engine, the solemnity of the moment hung in the air. Joginder Singh, standing tall, extended a wave of encouragement, his parting words a simple yet profound directive, "Majid, just give your best; that's it."

The echo of those words resonated in Majid's ears, infusing him with a sense of responsibility that went beyond the twists and turns of the race—it embraced the essence of giving his all to uphold the legacy of the Singh family.

The sun shone radiantly on the undulating landscape, painting the afternoon with hues of warmth and anticipation. A gentle breeze whispered through the air, carrying the scent of adventure over the mountainous terrain. The racing enthusiasts gathered, their excitement palpable as the engines roared to life.

Majid quickly changed into his safety suit and wore his helmet. The safety crew checked the cars to see if the drivers wore seatbelts. After a thorough check, they signalled them to line up for the race at the starting point.

Lined up along the starting point were five formidable racing cars. At the forefront, gleaming ominously, was Ravi Chandar's sleek black sports car — a manifestation of speed and supremacy. Beside it, radiating a vibrant energy, stood the Singh family's transformed Yellow Honda City, now a sports car ready to take on the challenge.

The atmosphere buzzed with a charged tension as the drivers, adrenaline coursing through their veins, revved their engines in sync with the collective heartbeat of the spectators. The sunlight danced on the polished surfaces of the vehicles, creating a dazzling spectacle against the backdrop of the majestic mountains.

The race kicked off with the explosive energy of a starting pistol, and Ravi Chandar catapulted from the starting line like a bullet, leaving a smoking trail behind.

In contrast, Majid's strategy dictated a cautious beginning, a deliberate choice given the known constraints of their car. As the other three vehicles zipped ahead, Majid lingered at the tail end, biding his time.

The plan was clear: overtake each opponent methodically. With every thrilling turn and acceleration on the mountainous slopes, Majid executed the strategy flawlessly, weaving through hairpin bends with a precision that belied their vehicle's limitations.

Gradually, he left the rearview of the third and then the second car behind, claiming the second spot with five laps to go.

Sensing Majid's ascent, Ravi Chandar decided to seize an unbeatable lead. The chase intensified, with Majid tailing closely but unable to make the decisive overtake.

Ravi, perhaps driven by the thrill of the race or the desire to outwit his competitor, led Majid dangerously close to the edges, testing both skill and nerve.

As the tension reached its zenith, Majid, well-versed in the nuances of the terrain, held back, waiting for the opportune moment.

Then, with only a few laps left, Ravi unveiled a trump card — a dashboard switch labelled '3X Nitro Power.' Activating it, he surged forward like a lightning bolt, extending the lead.

It seemed inevitable that Ravi would secure another victory. However, Majid wasn't one to concede defeat readily. In a dramatic twist, he, too, revealed a '3X Nitro Power' switch on his dashboard.

The two cars raced side by side, neck and neck. Confident of his impending triumph, Ravi signalled to Majid that he had one more nitro boost left for the last lap.

With an evil grin, Ravi activated his final nitro boost.

Yet, as he pressed the button, an unexpected turn of events unfolded. Majid shot past Ravi in unparalleled speed just moments before the finish line.

The mountain air crackled with the intensity of the race, and Majid, against all odds, emerged as the victor, leaving Ravi Chandar in disbelief.

The finish line witnessed not just a race but a triumph of strategy, skill, and a secret weapon that turned the tables in the final moments of an unforgettable mountain showdown.

The scene erupted in jubilation as Sarah, Tracy, and Vicky leapt with unbridled joy. Amidst the celebration,

Sarah exclaimed, "Majid saved the SuperCharge for the last!"

Jolly, observing the race through the lens of a video call, experienced a bittersweet moment. "With such an advanced car, I would have definitely won this year!" he remarked. Nevertheless, he couldn't help but feel elated that they had successfully outpaced Ravi Chandar.

The trio dashed toward the finish line, their excitement palpable. As Majid emerged from the victorious car, he removed his helmet, revealing a triumphant smile. With a hand raised towards the sky, he acknowledged the collective effort that had led to this triumph.

Walking towards the Singhs, the crowd surrounding them erupted into cheers, chanting, "Majid Schumacher! Majid Schumacher!" The moniker, a nod to the legendary racer Michael Schumacher, echoed through the mountains, encapsulating the essence of Majid's spectacular victory.

CHAPTER 19

Goodbye India!

The Singh household was alive with the vibrant celebration following Majid's triumph. Neetu and Yogesh, adding to the festivity, joined the Singhs on the subsequent day of the wedding ceremonies.

The Singh house's veranda became a hub of joy, adorned with an array of snacks, sweets, and jubilant conversations. Neetu's smile, already radiant with the glow of newlywed bliss, seemed to amplify in the light of Majid's victory. Adding to the joy, recently discharged Jolly made his way home, completing the familial circle.

In the joyous celebration, an inevitable moment of poignant farewell unfolded. Tracy and Sarah, integral threads woven into the fabric of the Singh family during their journey in India, stood at the crossroads of departure.

The air was thick with gratitude as they extended their sincere thanks to the Singhs, their extended family, Majid and Yogesh, for the enchanting time spent in the heart of India.

With folded hands, Tracy spoke a melodic blend of sincerity, "Joginder Singh Ji, you've given us moments that will forever reside in our lives. Thank you for embracing us as we are."

Tears welled up, bridging the departing guests and their gracious hosts. Neetu, Vicky, and Jolly implored, "Sarah and Tracy, please reconsider and extend your stay."

Tracy's reply was laden with a sense of duty and responsibility, "Our obligations beckon us back to the United States. We carry memories and the weight of fulfilling Tapinder's dream."

Joginder Singh Ji affirmed in his trademark tone, "Tracy and Sarah, this is your home; you can return anytime. We shall miss you dearly. Please come back soon."

Ever the witty soul, Sarah said, "Dadaji, I suggest you all visit the United States and witness the legacy your son has created. You'd be proud of his accomplishments!"

Tears glistened in Joginder Singh Ji and Amarjeet Kaur's eyes as they exchanged glances. Joginder Singh Ji vowed, "Yes, Sarah. We will visit you and witness our son's achievements."

Rekha added, "Tracy and Sarah, we'll miss you. I wish we had met earlier, not waiting for Tapinder's passing. Nonetheless, fate has its own course. We love you dearly, and your absence will leave a void in our hearts."

Tannu, with a soft cry, held Tracy's hand and adorned her wrist with a beautiful golden bracelet. "This will protect you Tracy, and empower you to face life's challenges."

Tracy embraced Tannu, appreciating the gesture. Neetu delicately removed a gold chain with a pearl pendant and placed it around Sarah's neck. Sarah bent to inspect it and reciprocated with a heartfelt hug.

Satpal and Kripashankar, holding a box of cherished memories, presented Tracy and Sarah with wooden toys from their childhood. "These belong to you now, part of the legacy we entrust to your care."

Inspired by Tapinder's memory and motivated by the warmth they received from the Singh family in Behalpur, Tracy and Sarah decided to immortalise his legacy through a noble initiative.

Tracy announced, "We've established the Tapinder Educational Fund. Joginder Singh Ji shall be its head. The primary goal is to enhance the educational infrastructure in Behalpur, aligning with Tapinder's vision for progress and empowerment through learning."

Touched by the gesture, Joginder Singh Ji graciously accepted their proposal. "Thank you for your kind gesture and generosity. It will help build Tapinder's legacy in Behalpur."

Amid farewells and tight hugs, promises were made to stay connected across continents, bridging the physical gap with the enduring bonds forged during these eventful days.

Sarah and Tracy prepared to embark on their return journey, with Majid driving them to the New Delhi Airport.

The time for departure had arrived, and the morning air was crisp as Tracy and Sarah, bags packed and ready, prepared to bid farewell to the Singh household.

Majid pulled up with Joginder Singh Ji's Merc, the same car that had brought them from New Delhi to Behalpur. The entire Singh family roused from their slumber to offer the departing duo warm goodbyes and heartfelt hugs.

As Majid revved the engine, Sarah and Tracy settled into the car, and with a burst of energy, Majid set off. After a seven-hour-long journey, they reached the airport, where Majid accompanied them, assisting with their luggage and bidding them farewell at the airport gate.

Majid's sadness at Sarah's departure was evident. A soft spot had developed, and he cherished the role of their tour guide.

Observing Majid's melancholic expression, Sarah interrupted the emotional moment and expressed her gratitude: "Majid, thank you so much for being our guide. Your support made our journey enjoyable and memorable. I will never forget you. I would love to keep in touch with you."

With these words, Sarah enveloped Majid in a tight hug, catching him by surprise and evoking a shy response reminiscent of a small-town boy.

With mischievous intent, Tracy prodded Sarah about a recent visit to the Wishing Pond in Behalpur. She reminded Sarah of a wish made after tossing a 10 Rupee coin.

Intrigued, Tracy asked, "Majid took us to that Wishing Pond in Behalpur a few days ago. Sarah, you had wished for something after throwing a 10 Rupee coin, right? Can you tell us now what you wished for?"

With a sheepish grin, Sarah confessed, "I wished for a chance for Majid to participate and win the mountain race!" The trio laughed, the shared joy echoing through the airport.

The sentiment lingered in the air, promising to stay connected across continents, leaving behind a trail of memories as they embarked on their separate journeys.

With final goodbyes, Sarah and Tracy offered to part words in unison, "Rev up the dreams, Majid Schumacher!"

www.ingramcontent.com/pod-product-compliance
Lightning Source LLC
Chambersburg PA
CBHW021959150726
47990CB00002B/516